Feeling a little foolish, she sat back down as Alexander started rowing. The moon was so bright ▮▮▮▮▮▮▮▮▮▮▮▮▮▮▮**cles of his arms bu**▮▮▮▮▮▮▮▮▮▮▮**of the oar.**

"Are we going to fish▮▮▮

"If you like. But later. I want to show you something first."

A comfortable silence fell, punctuated only by the creak of the boat against the oars and the lapping of the sea. Katherine trailed her hand in the water.

"Watch out for sharks," he cautioned.

She pulled her hand out of the water as if she'd had an electric shock. But when she looked at him she saw from his grin that he'd been teasing her.

Her skin tingled and she grinned back at him.

"So, what is it you want to show me?"

"I'm afraid you're going to have to wait and see."

He refused to say any more, so she let herself relax, gasping with delight as a shooting star sped across the sky before falling to the black depths of the ocean. It was as if she had been transported into a different world. Happiness surged through her. Everything about being here—being with Alexander—made her feel more alive than she'd ever felt before. As if the person she was when she was with him was a different, more together version of herself on one hand and a wilder, more interesting version on the other.

Dear Reader,

Many of you will know that I like to set my books in countries I love and where I have spent time, and this one is no exception.

The Peloponnese is perhaps less well-known than the Greek islands or Athens, but it has its own charm—stunning beaches, spectacular mountains (with very scary roads!), and around every corner a famous city, ruin or legend.

I hope you enjoy spending time with Alexander and Katherine, each of them with their own secret, as they track down the source of a meningitis epidemic while trying not to fall in love.

Anne Fraser

FALLING FOR DR. DIMITRIOU
ANNE FRASER

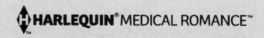
HARLEQUIN® MEDICAL ROMANCE™

Recycling programs
for this product may
not exist in your area.

ISBN-13: 978-0-373-06981-1

FALLING FOR DR. DIMITRIOU

First North American Publication 2014

Printed in U.S.A.

www.Harlequin.com

Recent titles by Anne Fraser:

THE WIFE HE NEVER FORGOT‡
CINDERELLA OF HARLEY STREET
HER MOTHERHOOD WISH**
THE FIREBRAND WHO UNLOCKED HIS HEART
MISTLETOE, MIDWIFE…MIRACLE BABY
DOCTOR ON THE RED CARPET
THE PLAYBOY OF HARLEY STREET
THE DOCTOR AND THE DEBUTANTE
DAREDEVIL, DOCTOR…DAD!†
MIRACLE: MARRIAGE REUNITED
SPANISH DOCTOR, PREGNANT MIDWIFE*

**The Most Precious Bundle of All
†St Piran's Hospital
*The Brides of Penhally Bay
‡Men of Honor

**These books are also available in ebook format
from www.Harlequin.com.**

PROLOGUE

IT WAS THAT moment before dawn, before the sky had begun to lighten and the moon seemed at its brightest, when Alexander saw her for the first time. On his way to the bay where he kept his boat, his attention was caught by a woman emerging like Aphrodite from the sea.

She paused, the waves lapping around her thighs, to squeeze the water from her tangled hair. As the sun rose, it bathed her in light adding to the mystical scene. He held his breath. He'd heard about her—in a village this size it would have been surprising if the arrival of a stranger wasn't commented on—and they hadn't exaggerated when they'd said she was beautiful.

The bay where she'd been swimming was below him, just beyond the wall that bordered the village square. If she looked up she would see him. But she didn't. She waded towards the shore, droplets clinging to her golden skin, her long hair still streaming with water. If the village hadn't been full of gossip about the woman who'd come to stay in the villa overlooking the bay, he could almost let himself believe that she was a mythical creature rising from the sea.

Almost. If he were a fanciful man. Which he wasn't.

CHAPTER ONE

KATHERINE PLACED HER pen on the table and leaned back in her chair. She picked up her glass of water, took a long sip and grimaced. It was tepid. Although she'd only poured it a short while ago, the ice cubes had already melted in the relentless midday Greek sun.

As it had done throughout the morning, her gaze drifted to the bay almost immediately below her veranda. The man was back. Over the last few evenings he'd come down to the little bay around five and stayed there, working on his boat until the sun began to set. He always worked with intense concentration, scraping away paint and sanding, stopping every so often to step back and evaluate his progress. But today, Saturday, he'd been there since early morning.

He was wearing jeans rolled up above his ankles and a white T-shirt that emphasised his golden skin, broad shoulders and well-developed biceps. She couldn't make out the colour of his eyes, but he had dark hair, curling on his forehead and slightly over his neckline. Despite what he was wearing, she couldn't help thinking of a Greek warrior—although there was nothing but gentleness in the way he treated his boat.

Who was he? she wondered idly. If her friend Sally were here she would have found out everything about him, down to his star sign. Unfortunately Katherine wasn't as gorgeous as Sally, to whom men responded like flies around a honey pot and who had always had some man on the go—at least until she'd met Tom. Now, insanely happily married to him, her friend had made it her mission in life to find someone for Katherine. So far her efforts had been in vain. Katherine had had her share of romances—well, two apart from Ben—but the only fizz in those had been when they'd fizzled out, and she'd given up on finding Mr Right a long time ago. Besides, men like the one she was watching were always attached to some beautiful woman.

He must have felt her eyes on him because he glanced up and looked directly at her. She scraped her chair back a little so that it was in the shadows, hoping that the dark glasses she was wearing meant he couldn't be sure she had been staring at him.

Not that she was at all interested in him, she told herself. It was just that he was a diversion from the work she was doing on her thesis—albeit a very pleasing-to-the-eye diversion.

Everything about Greece was a feast for the senses. It was exactly as her mother had described it—blindingly white beaches, grey-green mountains and a translucent sea that changed colour depending on the tide and the time of day. She could fully grasp, now, why her mother had spoken of the country of her birth so often and with such longing.

Katherine's heart squeezed. Was it already four weeks since Mum had died? It felt like only yesterday. The month had passed in a haze of grief and Katherine had worked even longer hours in an attempt to keep herself from thinking too much, until Tim, her boss, had pulled her aside and told her gently, but firmly, that she needed to take time off—especially as she hadn't had a holiday in years. Although she'd protested, he'd dug his heels in. Six weeks, he'd told her, and if he saw her in the office during that time, he'd call Security. One look at his face had told her he meant it.

Then when a work colleague had told her that the Greek parents of a friend of hers were going to America for the birth of their first grandchild and needed someone to stay in their home while they were away—someone who would care for their cherished cat and water the garden—Katherine knew it was serendipity; her thesis had been put to one side when Mum had been ill, and despite what Tim said about taking a complete rest, this would be the perfect time to finish it.

It would also be a chance to fulfil the promise she'd made to her mother.

The little whitewashed house was built on the edge of the village, tucked against the side of a mountain. It had a tiny open-plan kitchen and sitting room, with stone steps hewn out of the rock snaking up to the south-facing balcony that overlooked the bay. The main bedroom was downstairs, its door leading onto a small terrace that, in turn, led directly onto the beach. The garden was filled with pomegranate, fig and ancient, gnarled olive trees that provided much-needed shade. Masses of red bougainvillea, jasmine and honeysuckle clung to the wall, scenting the air.

The cat, Hercules, was no problem to look after. Most of the time he lay sunbathing on the patio and all she had to do was make sure he had plenty of water and feed him. She'd developed a fondness for him and he for her. He'd taken to sleeping on her bed and while she knew it was a habit she shouldn't encourage, there was something comforting about the sound of his purring and the warmth of his body curled up next to hers. And with that thought, her gaze strayed once more to the man working on the boat.

He'd resumed his paint scraping. He had to be hot down there where there was no shade. She wondered about offering him a drink. It would be the neighbourly, the polite thing to do. But she wasn't here to get to know the neighbours, she was here to see some of her mother's country and, while keeping her boss happy, to finish her thesis. Habits of a lifetime were too hard to break, though, and four days into her six-week holiday she hadn't actually seen very much of Greece, apart from a brief visit to the village her mother had lived as a child. Still, there was plenty of time and if she kept up this pace, her thesis would be ready to submit within the month and then she'd take time off to relax and sightsee.

However, the heat was making it difficult to concentrate. She should give herself a break and it wouldn't take her a moment to fetch him a drink. As it was likely he came from the village, he probably couldn't speak English very well anyway. That would definitely curtail any attempt to strike up a conversation.

Just as she stood to move towards the kitchen, a little girl, around five or six, appeared from around the corner of the cliff. She was wearing a pair of frayed denim shorts and a bright red T-shirt. Her long, blonde hair, tied up in a ponytail, bobbed as she skipped towards the man. A small spaniel, ears flapping, chased after her, barking excitedly.

'Baba!' she cried, squealing with delight, her arms waving like the blades of a windmill.

An unexpected and unwelcome pang of disappointment washed over Katherine. So he *was* married.

He stopped what he was doing and grinned, his teeth white against his skin.

'Crystal!' he said, holding his arms wide for the little girl to jump into them. Katherine could only make out enough of the rest of the conversation to know it was in Greek.

He placed the little girl down as a woman, slim with short blonde hair, loped towards them. This had to be the wife. She was carrying a wicker basket, which she laid on the sand, and said something to the man that made him grin.

The child, the cocker spaniel close on her

heels, ran around in circles, her laughter ringing through the still air.

There was something about the small family, their utter enjoyment of each other, the tableau they made, that looked so perfect it made Katherine's heart contract. This was what family life should be—might have been—but would likely never be. At least, not for her.

Which wasn't to say that she didn't love the life she did have. It was interesting, totally absorbing and worthwhile. Public health wasn't regarded as the sexiest speciality, but in terms of saving lives most other doctors agreed it was public-health doctors and preventive medicine that made the greatest difference. One only had to think about the Broad Street pump, for example. No one had been able to stop the spread of cholera that had raged through London in the 1800s until they'd found its source.

When she next looked up the woman had gone but the detritus of a picnic still remained on the blanket. The man was leaning against a rock, his long legs stretched out in front of him, the child, dwarfed by his size, snuggled into his side, gazing up at him with a rapt expression on her face as he read to her from a story book.

It was no use, she couldn't concentrate out here. Gathering up her papers, she went back inside. She'd work for another hour before stopping for lunch. Perhaps then she'd explore the village properly. Apart from the short trip to Mum's village—and what a disappointment that had turned out to be—she'd been too absorbed in her thesis to do more than go for a swim or a walk along the beach before breakfast and last thing at night. Besides, she needed to stock up on more provisions.

She'd been to the shop on the village square once to buy some tomatoes and milk and had had to endure the undisguised curiosity of the shopkeeper and her customers and she regretted not having learnt Greek properly when she'd had the chance to do so. Her mother had been a native Greek speaker but she had never spoken it at home and consequently Katherine knew little of the language.

However, she hated the way some tourists expected the locals to speak English, regardless of what country they found themselves in, and had made sure she'd learnt enough to ask for what she needed—at the very least, to say please, thank you and to greet people. In the store, she'd managed to ask for what she wanted through a combination of hand signals and her few words of Greek—the latter causing no small amount of amusement.

She glanced at her papers and pushed them away with a sigh. The warm family scene she'd witnessed had unsettled her, bringing back the familiar ache of loneliness and longing. Since her concentration was ruined, she may as well go to the village now. A quick freshen-up and then she'd be good to go. Walking into her bedroom, she hesitated. She crossed over to her bedside drawer and removed the photograph album she always kept with her. She flicked through the pages until she found a couple of photos of Poppy when she was six—around the same age as the little girl in the bay.

This particular one had been taken on the beach—Brighton, if she remembered correctly. Poppy was kneeling in the sand, a bucket and spade next to her, a deep frown knotting her forehead as she sculpted what looked like a very wobbly sandcastle. She was in a bright one-piece costume, her hair tied up in bunches on either side of her head. Another, taken the same day, was of Poppy in Liz's arms, the remains of an ice cream still evident on her face, her head thrown back as if she'd been snapped right in the middle of a fit of giggles. Katherine could see the gap in the front of her mouth where her baby teeth had fallen out, yet to be replaced with permanent ones. She appeared happy, blissfully so. As happy as the child she'd seen earlier.

She closed the album, unable to bear looking further. Hadn't she told herself that it was useless to dwell on what might have been? Work. That was what always stopped her dwelling on the past. The trip to the village could wait.

Immersed in her writing, Katherine was startled by a small voice behind her.

'*Yiássas.*'

Katherine spun around in her chair. She hadn't heard anyone coming up the rock steps but she instantly recognised the little girl from the bay. 'Oh, hello.' What was she doing here? And on her own? 'You gave me a bit of a fright,' she added in English.

The child giggled. 'I did, didn't I? I saw you earlier when I was with Baba. You were on the balcony.' She pointed to it. 'I don't think you have any friends so I thought you might want a visitor. Me!' Her English was almost perfect, although heavily accented.

Katherine laughed but it didn't sound quite as carefree as she hoped. 'Some adults like their own company.' She gestured to the papers in front of her. 'Besides, I have lots of work to do while I'm here.'

The girl studied her doubtfully for a few moments. 'But you wouldn't mind if I come and see you sometimes?'

What could she say to that? 'No, of course not. But I'm afraid you wouldn't find me very good company. I'm not used to entertaining little girls.'

The child looked astounded. 'But you must have been a little girl once! Before you got old.'

This time Katherine's laugh was wholehearted. 'Exactly. I'm old. No fun. Should you be here? Your family might be worried about you.'

The child's eyes widened. 'Why?'

'Well, because you're very small still and most of the time parents like to know where their children are and what they're up to.' She winced inwardly, aware of the irony of what she'd said.

'But they do know where I am, silly. I'm in the village! Hello, Hercules.' The girl knelt and stroked the cat. Suddenly pandemonium broke out. It seemed her spaniel had come to look for her. He ran into the room and spotting the cat made a beeline for it. With a furious yowl Hercules leapt up and onto Katherine's desk, scattering her papers, pens and pencils onto the floor. She grabbed and held on to the struggling cat as the dog jumped up against her legs, barking excitedly.

'Kato! Galen! Kato!' A stern male voice cut through the chaos. It was the child's father—the boat man. God, how many other people and animals were going to appear uninvited in her living room?

The spaniel obediently ran over to the man and lay down at his feet, tail wagging and panting happily. Now the father's censorious gaze rested on his little girl. After speaking a few words in Greek, he turned to Katherine. 'I apologise for my daughter's intrusion. She knows she shouldn't wander off without letting me know first. I didn't notice she'd gone until I saw her footprints headed this way.' His English was impeccable with only a trace of an attractive accent. 'Please, let us help you gather your papers.'

Close up he was overwhelmingly good-looking, with thick-lashed sepia eyes, a straight nose, curving sensual mouth and sharp cheekbones. Katherine felt another stab of envy for the blonde-haired woman. She lowered the still protesting Hercules to the floor. With a final malevolent glance at the spaniel, he disappeared outside.

'Please, there's no need…'

But he was already picking up some of the strewn papers. 'It's the least we can do.'

Katherine darted forward and placed a hand on his arm. To her dismay, her fingertips tingled where they touched his warm skin and she quickly snatched it away. 'I'd rather you didn't—they might get even more muddled up.'

He straightened and studied her for a moment from beneath dark brows. He was so close she could smell his soap and almost feel waves of energy pulsating from him. Every nerve cell in her body seemed to be on alert, each small hair on her body standing to attention. Dear God, that she should be reacting like this to a married man! What the hell was wrong with her? She needed to get a grip. 'Accidents happen, there is no need for you to do anything, thank you,' she said. Thankfully her voice sounded normal.

'Yes, Baba! Accidents happen!' the little girl piped up in English.

His response to his daughter, although spoken softly in Greek, had her lowering her head again, but when he turned back to Katherine a smile lighted his eyes and played around the corners of his mouth. He raked a hand through his hair. 'Again I must apologise for my daughter. I'm afraid Crystal is too used to going in and out of all the villagers' homes here and doesn't quite understand that some people prefer to offer invitations.'

Crystal looked so woebegone that Katherine found herself smiling back at them. 'It's fine—I needed a break. So now I'm having one—a little earlier than planned, but that's okay.'

'In which case we'll leave you to enjoy it in peace.' He glanced at her ringless fingers. 'Miss...?'

'Burns. Katherine Burns.'

'Katherine.' The way he rolled her name around his mouth made it sound exotic. 'And I am Alexander Dimitriou. I've noticed you watching from your balcony.'

'Excuse me! I wasn't watching you! I was working on my laptop and you just happened to be directly in my line of sight whenever I lifted my head.' The arrogance of the man! To take it for granted that she'd been watching him— even if she had.

When he grinned she realised she'd let him know that she had noticed him. The way he was looking at her was disturbing. It was simply not right for a married man to look at a woman who wasn't his wife that way.

'Perhaps,' he continued, 'you'll consider joining my family one day for lunch, to make up for disrupting your day?'

She wasn't here to hang around divine-looking Greek men—particularly married ones! 'Thank you,' she responded tersely. 'I did say to Crystal that she could come and visit me again some time,' she added as she walked father and daughter outside, 'but perhaps you should remind her to let you know before she does?'

She stood on the balcony, watching as they ambled hand in hand across the beach towards the village square, Crystal chattering and swinging on her father's arm. Even from this distance she could hear his laughter. With a sigh she turned around and went back inside.

Later that evening, after Crystal was in bed, Alexander's thoughts returned to Katherine, as they had over the last few days—ever since the morning he'd seen her come out of the water. It was just his luck that the villa she was staying in overlooked the bay where he was working on his boat.

He couldn't help glancing her way as she sat on her balcony, her head bent over her laptop as she typed, pausing only to push stray locks from her eyes—and to watch him.

And she *had* been watching him. He'd looked up more than once to catch her looking in his direction. She'd caused quite a stir in the vil-

lage, arriving here by herself. The villagers, his
grandmother and cousin Helen included, continued to be fascinated by this woman who'd
landed in their midst and who kept herself to
herself, seldom venturing from her temporary
home unless it was to have a quick dip in the sea
or shop for groceries at the village store. They
couldn't understand anyone coming on holiday
by themselves and had speculated wildly about
her.

To their disappointment she hadn't stopped
for a coffee or a glass of wine in the village
square or to try some of Maria's—the owner
of only taverna in the village—home-cooked
food so there had been no opportunity to find
out more about her. Helen especially would have
loved to know more about her—his cousin was
always on at him to start dating again.

But, despite the fact Katherine was undeni-
ably gorgeous, he wasn't interested in long-term
relationships and he had the distinct impression
that Miss Burns didn't do short-term ones.

However, there was something about this
particular woman that drew him. Perhaps, he
thought, because he recognised the same sadness in her that was in him. All the more reason, then, for him to keep his distance.

CHAPTER TWO

THE NEXT MORNING, having decided to work inside and out of sight, Katherine only managed to resist for a couple of hours before finding herself drawn like a magnet to the balcony.

Gazing down at the beach, she saw that Alexander, stripped to the waist, his golden skin glistening with a sheen of perspiration, was back working on his boat again. Dragging her gaze away from him, she closed her eyes for a moment and listened to the sound of the waves licking the shore. The sweet smell of oranges from a nearby orchard wafted on the breeze. Being here in Greece was like a balm for her soul.

A sharp curse brought her attention back to the bay.

Alexander had dropped his paint-scraper. He studied his hand for a moment and shook his head. He looked around as if searching for a bandage, but apparently finding only his T-shirt, bent to pick it up, and wound it around his palm.

She could hardly leave him bleeding—especially when, prepared as always, she'd brought a small first-aid kit with her and it was unlikely there would be a doctor available on a Sunday in such a small village.

The blood had pretty much soaked through his temporary bandage by the time she reached him but, undaunted, he had carried on working, keeping his left hand—the damaged one—elevated in some kind of optimistic hope of stemming the bleeding.

'*Kaliméra!*' Katherine called out, not wanting to surprise him. When he looked up, she pointed to his hand and lifted the first-aid kit she carried. 'Can I help?'

'It's okay, I'll manage,' he replied. When he smiled, her heart gave a queer little flutter. 'But thank you.'

'At least let me look at it. Judging by the amount of blood, you've cut it pretty badly.'

His smile grew wider. 'If you insist,' he said, holding out his injured hand.

She drew closer to him and began unwrapping his makeshift bandage. As she gently tugged the remaining bit of cloth aside and her fingers encountered the warmth of his work-roughened palm, she felt the same frisson of electricity course through her body as she had the day before. Bloody typical; the first time she could remember meeting someone whom she found instantly attractive he had to be married—and a father to boot.

'It's deep,' she said, examining the wound, 'and needs stitches. Is there a surgery open today?'

'Most of them are open for emergencies only on a Sunday. I'm not sure this constitutes one.'

'I think it does.' Katherine said, aware that her tone sounded schoolmistress prim. 'I'm a doctor, so I do know what I'm talking about.'

His eyebrows shot up. 'Are you really? The villagers had you down as a writer. A GP, I take it?'

Katherine shook her head. 'No. Epidemiology. Research. I'm in public health.'

'But not on holiday? You seemed pretty immersed in paperwork yesterday.'

'My thesis. For my PhD.'

'Brains too.' He grinned. 'So can't you stitch my hand?'

'Unfortunately, no. I could if I had a suturing kit with me but I don't. Anyway, you'll likely need a tetanus shot unless you've had one recently. Have you?'

'No.'

For some reason, the way he was looking at

her made her think that he was laughing at her. 'Then one of the emergency surgeries it will have to be,' she said firmly. 'I'll clean and bandage the cut in the meantime. Is there someone who can give you a lift?'

'No need—it's within walking distance. Anyway, this little scratch is not going to kill me.'

'Possibly not but it could make you very sick indeed.' She thought for a moment. 'I strongly advise you to find out whether the doctor is willing to see you. I'll phone him if you like. As one doctor to another, he might be persuaded to see you.'

He was no longer disguising his amusement. 'Actually, that would be a bit embarrassing seeing as I'm the doctor and it's my practice—one of them anyway.'

'You're a doctor?' She couldn't keep the surprise out of her voice. She felt more than slightly foolish, standing before him with her little plastic medical kit. If he was a GP he was probably more qualified than she to assess the damage to his hand. Now she knew the reason for his secret amusement. 'You might have mentioned this before,' she continued through gritted teeth.

Alexander shrugged. 'I was going to, I promise. Eventually.' That smile again. 'I suppose I was enjoying the personal attention—it's nice to be on the receiving end for a change.'

'You really should have said straight away,' she reiterated, struggling to control the annoyance that was rapidly replacing her embarrassment. 'However, you can hardly suture your hand yourself.' Although right this minute she was half-minded to let him try.

'I could give it a go,' he replied, 'but you're right, it would be easier and neater if you did it. The practice I have here is really little more than a consulting room I use when the older villagers need to see a doctor and aren't unwell enough to warrant a trip to my practice. But it's reasonably well equipped. You could stitch it there.'

'In that case, lead the way.'

His consulting room had obviously once been a fisherman's cottage, with the front door leading directly onto the village square. There were only two rooms leading off the small hall and he opened the door to the one on the left. It was furnished with an examination couch, a stainless-steel trolley, a sink and most of what she'd expect to find in a small rural surgery. The one surprise was a deep armchair covered with a throw. He followed her gaze and grimaced. 'I know that doesn't really belong, but my older patients like to feel more at home when they come to see me here.'

Not really the most sanitary of arrangements, but she kept her own counsel. It wasn't up to her to tell him how to run his practice.

He opened a cupboard and placed some local anaesthetic and a syringe on the desk, along with a disposable suture tray. He perched on the couch and rested his hand, palm up, on his leg.

He definitely has the physique of a gladiator, she thought, her gaze lingering on his chest for a moment too long. She shifted her gaze and found him looking at her, one eyebrow raised and a small smile playing on his lips. As heat rushed to her cheeks she turned away, wishing she'd left him to deal with his hand himself.

She washed her hands and slipped on a pair of disposable gloves, acutely conscious of his teasing appraisal as she filled the syringe with the local anaesthetic. Studiously avoiding looking at his naked chest, she gently lifted up his hand and, after swabbing the skin, injected into the wound. He didn't even flinch as she did so. 'I'll wait a few minutes for it to take effect.'

'So what brings you here?' he asked. 'It isn't one of the usual tourists spots.'

'I was kindly offered the use of the Dukases' villa through a colleague who is a friend of their daughter in exchange for taking care of Hercules and the garden. My mother was from Greece and I've always wanted to see the country where she was born.'

'She was from here?'

'From Ītylo. This was the closest I could get to there.'

'It's your first time in the Peloponnese?'

'My first time in Greece,' Katherine admitted.

'And your mother didn't come with you?'

'No. She passed away recently.' To her dismay, her voice hitched. She swallowed the lump in her throat before continuing. 'She always wanted the two of us to visit Greece together, but her health prevented her from travelling. She had multiple sclerosis.'

'I'm sorry.' Two simple words, but the way he said it, she knew he really meant it.

She lightly prodded his palm with her fingertips. 'How does that feel?'

'Numb. Go ahead.'

Opening up the suture pack, she picked up the needle. Why did he have to be nice as well as gorgeous?

'I hope you're planning to see some of the Peloponnese while you're here. Olympia? Delphi? Athens and the Acropolis for sure. The city of Mycenae, perhaps?'

Katherine laughed. 'They're all on my list. But I want to finish my thesis first.'

He raised his head and frowned slightly. 'So no holiday for a while, then? That's not good. Everyone needs to take time out to relax.'

'I do relax. Often.' Not that often—but as often as she wanted to. 'Anyway I find work relaxing.'

'Mmm,' he said, as if he didn't believe her. Or approve. 'Work can be a way to avoid dealing with the unbearable. Not good for the psyche if it goes on too long. You need to take time to grieve,' he suggested gently.

She stiffened. Who was he to tell her what was good for her and what she needed? How he chose to live his life was up to him, just as it was up to her how she lived.

'I must apologise again for yesterday,' he continued, when she didn't reply, 'You were obviously working so I hope we didn't set you back too much. My daughter's been dying to meet you since you arrived. I'm afraid her curiosity about you got the better of her.'

Katherine inserted a stitch and tied it off. 'Your daughter is charming and very pretty.'

'Yes, she is. She takes after her mother.'

'I take it the beautiful woman on the beach yesterday is your wife?' she said, inserting another l stitch.

When she heard his sharp intake of breath she stopped. 'I'm sorry. Did that hurt? Didn't I use enough local?'

His expression was taut, but he shook his head. 'I can't feel a thing. The woman you saw is Helen, my cousin. My wife died.'

Katherine was appalled. 'I'm so sorry. How awful for you and your daughter. To lose her mother when so young.' She winced inwardly at her choice of words.

'Yes,' he said abruptly. 'It was.'

So he knew loss too. She bent her head again and didn't raise it until she'd added the final stitch and the wound was closed. When had his wife died? Crystal had to be, what? Four? Five? Therefore it had to be within that time frame. Judging by the bleakness in his eyes, the loss was still raw. In which case he might as well be married. And why the hell were her thoughts continuing along this route?

She gave herself a mental shake and placed a small square dressing on top and finished with a bandage, pleased that her work was still as neat as it had been when she'd sutured on a regular basis.

'What about tetanus?' she asked. 'I'm assuming you have some in stock here?'

'Suppose I'd better let you give me that too. It's been over five years since I last had one.' He went to the small drugs fridge and looked inside. 'Hell,' he said after examining the contents. 'I'm out. Never mind, I'll get it when I go back to my other surgery tomorrow.'

'It could be too late by then—as I'm sure you know. No, since it seems that you are my patient, at least for the moment, I'm going to have to insist you get one today.'

He eyed her. 'That would mean a trip to Pýrgos—almost an hour from here. Unfortunately, Helen has taken my car to take Crystal to play with a friend and won't be back until tonight. Tomorrow it will have to be.'

She hesitated, but only for a moment. 'In that case, I'll drive you.'

'Something tells me you're not going to back down on this.'

She smiled. 'And you'd be right.' She arched an eyebrow. 'You might want to fetch a clean shirt. Why don't you do that while I get my car keys?'

But it seemed as if she'd offered him a lift without the means to carry it through. Not wanting

to drive down from Athens —she'd heard about
the Peloponnese roads, especially the one that
ran between here and the Greek capital—she'd
taken a circuitous route; first an early morning
flight, followed by a ferry and then two buses
to the rental company In hindsight it would have
been quicker and probably far less stressful to
have flown into Athens.

And now she had a puncture. Thankfully the
car did have a spare wheel. She jacked it up and
found the wrench to loosen the bolts but they
wouldn't budge. No doubt they had rusted.

'Problems?'

She whirled around to find Alexander standing behind her. He had showered and changed
into light-coloured cotton trousers and a white
short-sleeved shirt.

'Puncture. I'm just changing the wheel. As
soon as I get a chance, I'm going to exchange
this heap for something better.'

The car the company had given her had more
dents and bashes in it than a rally car after a
crash. She would have insisted on a newer, more
pristine model, but the company had said it was
the only one they had available.

His lips twitched. He walked around the car,
shaking his head. 'They palmed this off on you?'

'Yes, well, I was tired.' She resented the fact

that he thought she'd let herself be taken advantage of—even if she had.

'Which company did you rent this from?'

She told him.

'In that case, they have a branch in Katákolo, which isn't too far from where we're going.'

'Will it be open on a Sunday?'

'The cruise ships all offer day trips to Olympia from there. Like most places that cater for tourists, everything will be open. Once I've been jagged to your satisfaction I'll make sure they exchange it for something better.'

'I'm perfectly able to manage to sort it out myself.' Did all Greek men think women were helpless?

He drew back a little, holding up his hands. 'Hey. You're helping me. And it's not far from where we're going.'

She was instantly ashamed of herself. He'd done nothing to warrant her snapping at him. It was hardly his fault that he made her feel like a schoolgirl with her first crush.

'I'm sorry. It's just that I'm a bit hot.' She sought a better reason to excuse her behaviour, but apart from telling him that he found his company unsettling she couldn't think of one. 'In the meantime, I still have to change the wheel.' She picked up a rock and hit the wrench. Nothing. No movement. Not even a centimetre.

He crouched down next to her, the muscles of his thighs straining against the material of his trousers. 'Let me do it.'

'I can manage. At least I would if the things weren't stuck.'

He took the wrench from her. 'It just needs a little strength.'

'You shouldn't. Not with your hand recently sutured.'

He ignored her and within moments the nuts were off the wheel. He took the flat tyre off and silently she passed him the spare.

'I probably loosened them.' He looked up at her and grinned. 'I'm sure you did.' He lifted the new wheel into position and replaced the bolts.

'Thank you,' she said. 'I can take it from here.'

He stood back and watched as she lowered the car to the ground.

'I'll just tighten the bolts again,' he said, 'then we'll be good to go. Would you like me to drive?'

'No, thank you.'

Despite the open windows the car was hot; unsurprisingly, the air-conditioning didn't work either. Katherine gripped the steering-wheel, trying not to flinch whenever a car overtook her, the vehicle often swerving back in just in time to avoid being smashed into by another coming in the opposite direction. Perhaps she should have taken Alexander up on his offer to drive? But if he drove the same way as his country-men did, being a passenger would be ten times worse. She preferred being in control.

Eventually the countryside gave way to denser traffic and by the time Alexander directed her to a parking spot in front of the surgery she was a nervous wreck, her hands were damp and she knew her hair was plastered to her scalp. She was beginning to appreciate why the car the company had given her was badly dented.

He looked relieved as he undid his seat belt. 'This won't take long but why don't you go for a walk while you're waiting?'

'If you're going to be quick I might as well come in with you.' She was curious to see how the medical services in Greece worked.

While Alexander greeted the receptionist, Katherine took a seat in the small waiting room next to an elderly woman with a bandage on her knee and clutching a walking stick. Alexander turned to her and said something in Greek that made her laugh.

'Mrs Kalfas is waiting for her husband to collect her,' he explained to Katherine, 'so I can go straight in. I won't be long.'

A few moments after Alexander disappeared from sight, a man in his early to mid-twenties, staggered in and, after saying a few words to the receptionist, almost fell into one of the empty chairs. He was good-looking with dark curly hair, a full mouth and olive skin, but his jeans and checked shirt were stained and crumpled as if he'd picked them up off the bedroom floor, too ill to care. His cheeks were flushed and his eyes, when he managed to open them briefly, glittered with fever. Perhaps she should have gone for that walk. All doctors knew that hospitals and GP waiting rooms were bad news for the healthy.

Mrs Kalfas tried to strike up a conversation with him, but he appeared to have little interest in whatever she was saying. Warning bells started to clamour in Katherine's head as she studied him covertly from under her eyelids. Now she wondered if his eyes were closed because the light was annoying him—and the way he kept pressing his hand to the back of his neck as if it were sore alarmed her too. He really didn't look well at all. The receptionist should have let the doctors know that he was here.

Katherine was about to suggest it when he gave a loud moan and slid to the floor. Instantly she was on her feet and, crouching by his side, feeling for his pulse. It was there but weak and rapid. She glanced around but annoyingly there was no sign of the receptionist. Mrs Kalfas was staring, horrified.

'I need some help here,' Katherine called out. 'Alexander!'

The door behind which he'd vanished was flung open and Alexander, followed by a short, balding, overweight man with a stethoscope wrapped around his neck, rushed over and knelt by Katherine's side.

'What happened?' Alexander asked.

'He came in a few minutes ago. I was just about to suggest he be taken through when he collapsed. He's been rubbing his neck as if it's painful or stiff. We should consider meningitis.'

Alexander and his colleague exchanged a few words in rapid Greek and the other doctor hurried away.

The man on the floor groaned softly. The receptionist reappeared and came to stand next to Mrs Kalfas, placing a comforting arm around the older woman. Alexander said something to the younger woman and she hurried back to her desk and picked up the phone.

'It could be a number of things but to be on the safe side Carlos—Dr Stavrou—is going to get a line so we can start him on IV antibiotics,' Alexander told Katherine. 'Diane is phoning for an ambulance.'

Carlos returned and ripped open a pack and handed Alexander a venflon. He quickly inserted it into a vein and, taking the bag of saline from his colleague, attached one end of the tube to the needle. When Katherine held out her hand for the bag of saline, Alexander passed it to her and she held it up so that the fluid could flow unimpeded. In the meantime, Alexander had injected antibiotics straight into one of the stricken patient's veins.

As Katherine placed an oxygen mask over his face, she was vaguely aware that the receptionist had returned and along with Mrs Kalfas was watching intently. Alexander whirled around and spoke rapidly to the receptionist. He translated her reply for Katherine.

'Diane says the ambulance will be here shortly. She's agreed to take Mrs Kalfas home instead of making her wait for her husband. Seeing she's had a bit of a fright, I think it's better.'

Katherine was impressed with the way he'd considered the old woman, even in the midst of an emergency. Their patient was still unconscious but apart from keeping an eye on his airway there was little more they could do until the ambulance arrived. They couldn't risk taking him in a car in case he arrested.

'You have a defib to hand?' she asked.

'Naturally.'

She wondered what had caused the man to collapse. A number of possibilities ran through her head, meningitis being one, but without further tests it was impossible to know. All they could do now was stabilise him until they got him to hospital.

Diane picked up her handbag and helped the old lady out. Soon after, the ambulance arrived and the paramedics took over. They spoke to Alexander before quickly loading the patient into the ambulance.

'Should one of us go with him?' Katherine asked.

'No need. Carlos wants to go. He's his patient.'

The ambulance doors were slammed shut and it drove away, sirens screaming.

'Are you all right?' Alexander asked.

'Perfectly. Could you make sure they test him for meningitis?'

'Bit of a leap, isn't it? Carlos said Stefan—the patient—is not only accident prone but there's a few bugs doing the rounds. Besides, I didn't see any signs of a rash.'

'Trust me. Communicable diseases are my area of expertise and that young man has all the signs—sensitivity to light, fever, neck pain. The rash could appear at any time.' Alexander studied her for a moment. 'It couldn't hurt to do a lumbar puncture. I'll phone the hospital and make sure they do all the tests. At least he's been started on IV antibiotics. In the meantime, I'm afraid we're going to have to wait here until Carlos returns. Is that okay?'

'Sure.' She smiled at him. 'You can show me around while we wait.'

The practice was as well equipped as any Katherine had seen. In addition to four consulting rooms, one for each of the doctors, one for the nurses and one for their physio, there was an X-ray room and a sleek, spotlessly clean treatment room. All the equipment was modern and up to date.

'You appear to be almost as well set up as a small hospital,' Katherine said, impressed.

'We never know what we're going to get, so we like to be prepared for the worst. We have, as you can imagine, a fair share of road traffic accidents on these roads and sometimes people bring the casualties here as it's closer than the hospital.' Not quite the small family practice she'd imagined.

'We don't do much more than stabilise them and send them on,' Alexander continued, 'but it can make the difference between survival and death.'

'You have advanced life-support training, then?'

'Yes. We all do. It also helps that I used to be a surgeon.' He picked up the phone. 'Would you excuse me while I phone the hospital?' he said. 'I need to tell them to watch out for meningitis, as you suggested, and Carlos was telling me earlier that one of my patients was admitted there last night. I'd like to find out how he's doing.'

'Be my guest,' Katherine replied. As she waited for him to finish the call she studied him covertly from under her lashes. The more she learned about him the more he intrigued her. So he used to be a surgeon. What, then, had brought him to what, despite the expensive and up-to-date equipment, was still essentially a rural family practice? Had he come back here because of his wife? And how had she died? Had she been a road traffic victim?

While he'd been talking on the phone, Alexander's expression had darkened. He ended the phone call and sat lost in thought for a while. It was almost as if he'd forgotten she was there.

'Something wrong?' she asked.

'The patient Carlos was telling me about has been transferred to a hospital in Athens. The hospital doctor who admitted him yesterday sent him there this morning, but he's left to go fishing and can't be reached. None of the staff on duty today can tell me anything.' He leaned back in his chair. 'I'll speak to him tomorrow and find out why he felt a transfer was necessary.' He shook his head as if to clear it. 'But I have spoken to the doctor on call today about Stéfan. She's promised to do a lumbar puncture on him.'

'Good,' Katherine said.

'So what is your thesis on?' Alexander asked.

'As I said, communicable diseases. Mainly African ones.'

'What stage of your training are you?'

She raised an eyebrow. 'Consultant. Have been for four years. I'm thinking of applying for a professor's post. Hence the doctorate.'

He whistled between his teeth. 'You're a consultant! You don't look old enough.'

'I'm thirty-four.'

They chatted for a while about her work and different infectious diseases Alexander had come across in Greece. Caught up in discussing her passion, she was surprised when she heard footsteps and Carlos came in. She'd no idea so much time had passed.

'How is our patient?' Alexander asked in English, after formally introducing her to his partner.

'His blood pressure had come up by the time I left him in the care of the emergency team at the hospital. They'll let me know how he is as soon as they've done all the tests.'

'Will you let me know when they do?'

'Of course.'

Alexander pushed away from the desk and stood. He smiled at Katherine. 'In that case, let's go and swap that car of yours.'

The car rental company did have another car for her, but it wouldn't be available until later that afternoon.

Katherine turned to Alexander. 'I'm sure you want to get home. Isn't there another rental company in the area?'

'I suspect you'll find the same thing there. The cruise ships come in in the morning and a lot of the passengers—those who don't want to take the bus tour to Olympia—hire a car for the day. They tend to bring them back around four.'

'Damn. That's three hours away.'

'We could have lunch,' he suggested. 'Or, if you're not hungry, we can go to Olympia ourselves. It's years since I've been and it's less than thirty minutes from here. By the time we get back, Costa here should have a car for you.' He smiled. 'You're in Greece now. You'll find life a lot easier if you accept that here time works in a different zone.'

She hid a sigh. She should be getting back to her thesis. By taking the morning off she risked falling behind the schedule she'd mapped out for herself.

Whoa—what was she thinking? Had she completely lost it? He was right. What was the hurry anyway? It was Sunday and an interesting, *single* hunk was wanting to spend time with her.

'I would love to see Olympia,' she said. And she would. It was near the top of her list of places to visit. It would also be less intense, less like a date, than having lunch.

'Good. That's settled, then.' He opened the passenger door for Katherine. She looked at him and arched an eyebrow.

'I think it will be less stressful—and safer for us all—if I drive,' he said. 'I know the roads better.'

She hesitated, then broke into a smile. 'To be honest, if I never have to drive that heap of scrap again it would be too soon. So be my guest. Knock yourself out.'

It wasn't long before she was regretting her decision—and her words. As far as she was concerned, Alexander drove just like every other Greek driver.

'When I said knock yourself out,' she hissed, 'I didn't mean literally.'

He laughed. 'Don't worry. I promise you driving this way is safer.'

Nevertheless, she was hugely relieved when they arrived still in one piece. Alexander found a space in the crowded car park.

'There are two parts to the site—the ruins of the ancient city and the museum. I suggest we start off in the museum, which is air-conditioned.' He glanced at her appraisingly and his lips twitched. She was wearing navy trousers and a white cotton blouse with a Peter Pan collar, which, she had to admit, while neat and professional were almost unbearably hot. 'It'll be cooler by the time we're finished. If I remember correctly, there is very little shade in the ruins.'

She wandered around the exhibits, trying to concentrate but not really able to. She was too acutely aware of the similarity between the physiques of the naked statues and the man close by.

When they'd finished in the museum they walked across to the ruins. Although it was cooler than it had been earlier, it was still hot and almost immediately she felt a trickle of perspiration gather between her breasts. Alexander, on the other hand, looked as fresh and as cool as he'd done since they'd left the village.

As he pointed out the temples of Zeus and Hera, Katherine began to relax. Perhaps it was because, away from the statues, she could concentrate on what Alexander was saying. He knew a great deal about Greek history and was an easy and informative guide and soon she was caught up in his stories about what life must have been like during the Ottoman era.

When they'd finished admiring the bouleuterion, where the statue of Zeus had once stood, he led her across to the track where the athletes had competed. 'Did you know they competed in the nude?'

Instantly an image of Alexander naked leaped into her head and blood rushed to her cheeks. She hoped he would think it was the heat that was making her flush but when she saw the amusement in his eyes she knew he was perfectly aware what she'd been thinking.

It was nuts. After Ben she'd only ever had one other significant long-term relationship— with Steven, one of her colleagues. When that had ended, after he'd been offered a job in the States, she'd been surprisingly relieved. Since then, although she'd been asked out many times and Sally had tried to fix her up with several of the unattached men she or Tom knew, and she'd gone out with two or three of them, no one had appealed enough to make her want to see them again beyond a couple of dates.

Relationships, she'd decided, were overrated. Many women were single and very happy— as was she. She could eat when she liked, go where she pleased without having to consult anyone, holiday where it suited her and work all weekend and every weekend if she wanted to. Until her mother's death, she had rarely been lonely—she hadn't lied to Crystal when she'd told her she preferred being on her own, but that didn't mean she didn't miss physical contact. That didn't mean she didn't miss sex.

She felt her flush deepen. But sex without strings had never been her cup of tea.

God! She'd thought more about sex over these last two days than she had in months. But it was hard *not* to think about it around all these nude statues. Perhaps it hadn't been such a good idea choosing to come here instead of lunch. Lunch might have been the safer option after all.

A replacement car still wasn't available when they returned to the rental company.

'Really!' Katherine muttered. 'It's almost six.' Unlike Alexander, she needed to cool off, preferably with an ice-cold shower. And to do that she needed to get home— –and out of Alexander's company.

'He promises he'll have one by seven. If not, he'll give you his own car.' Alexander grinned. 'I did warn you about Greek timing.'

'But aren't you in a hurry to get back?' she asked, dismayed. 'I mean, you've given up the best part of your day to help me out. You must have other stuff you'd rather be doing. And I should get back to my thesis.'

'Nope. I'm in no rush. As I said, I'm not expecting my cousin and Crystal home until later. And surely you can give yourself a few more hours off?' The laughter in his eyes dimmed momentarily. 'Trust me, sometimes work should take a back seat.'

It was all right for him, he clearly found it easy to relax. But to spend more time in his company, blushing and getting tongue-tied, was too embarrassing. Still, she couldn't very well make him take a taxi all the way back home—

even if it was an appealing thought. Maybe *she* should get a taxi home? Now she was being ridiculous! She was behaving like someone with sunstroke. She almost sighed with relief. Perhaps that was it? She clearly wasn't herself. She realised he was watching her curiously. What had he been saying? Oh, yes—something about dinner.

'In that case, dinner would be lovely,' she replied, pulling herself together. 'Do you have somewhere in mind?'

'As a matter of fact I do. It's down by the shore. They sell the best seafood this side of Greece.' He tilted his head. 'You do like seafood, don't you?'

'I love it.'

'Good. We can wave goodbye to the cruise ships and more or less have the place to ourselves. We'll leave the car here. It's not far.'

They walked along the deserted main street. Without the hordes of visitors and now that the shopkeepers had brought in their stands that had been filled with tourist souvenirs, maps and guides, the town had a completely different feel to it. It was as if it were a town of two identities—the one belonging to the tourists, and this typically Greek sleepy one.

The restaurant was situated at the end of a

quiet cul-de-sac and it didn't look very prepossessing from the rear, where the entrance was situated. Understated was the word Katherine would use to describe the interior with its striped blue and white table runners and unlit candles rammed into empty wine bottles. But when they were guided to a table on the veranda by the *maître d'*, the view took Katherine's breath away. White sands and a blue, blue sea glittered as if some ancient god had scattered diamonds onto its surface. Alexander pulled out a chair for her beneath the shade of a tree and she sank happily into it.

When Alexander chose the lobster, freshly caught that morning, she decided to have it too. And since he was determined to drive they ordered a glass of chilled white wine for her and a fruit juice for himself.

They chatted easily about Greece and the recent blow to its economy and Alexander suggested various other places she might want to visit. Then he asked which medical school she'd studied at and she'd told him Edinburgh. Surprisingly, it turned out that it had been one of his choices but in the end he'd decided on Bart's.

'What made you decide to study in England?' she asked.

'I was brought up there. My mother was from Kent.' That explained his excellent English.

'So you have a Greek father and an English mother. I'm the opposite. How did your parents meet?'

'My mother met my father when she was working in a taverna while she was backpacking around Greece. It was supposed to be her gap year but in the end she never made it to university. Not long after she and my father started dating, they married. They moved to an apartment in Athens and after a couple of years they had me, then my younger brother. But she always pined for England. My father lectured in archaeology so he applied for a post at the British Museum and when he was accepted, we upped and left. I was five at the time.

'My father always missed Greece, though, so we came back as a family whenever we could, particularly to see my grandmother—my father's mother—and all the other family—aunts and uncles and cousins. Greece has always felt like home to me. Dad died when he was in his early forties. My grandfather died shortly after he did and, as my father's eldest son, I inherited the villa I live in now, as well as the land around it. It's been in our family for generations. Naturally my grandmother still lives in the family home.'

Katherine wanted to ask about his wife, but judging by his terse response in the village consulting room earlier that was a no-go area. 'And where's your mother now?' she asked instead, leaning back as their waiter placed their drinks in front of them.

'Still in England,' Alexander continued, when their waiter had left. 'She hasn't been back since my father died. I don't think she can bear to come anymore. She lives close to my brother in Somerset.'

'Doesn't she miss her grandchild?'

'Of course. However, Mother's life is in England—it's where her friends and my brother and his family are. We visit her often and, of course, there's video chat.' He took a sip of his drink. 'That's enough about me. What about you? Is there someone waiting for you in the UK?'

'No. No one.'

He looked surprised. 'Divorced, then? I'm assuming no children otherwise they'd be with you.'

She hesitated. 'Not divorced. Never married.' She swallowed. 'And no children.'

'Brothers and sisters? Your dad?'

'My dad passed away when I was fifteen. And no brothers or sisters.'

'So an only child. Being on your own must have made your mother's death even harder to handle, then,' he said softly.

The sympathy in his voice brought a lump to her throat. But she didn't want him to feel sorry for her.

'As I told Crystal, I like my own company. I have loads of friends in the UK when—if—I feel the need to socialise.'

'No one who could come with you? We Greeks find it difficult to imagine being on our own. As you've probably noticed, we like to surround ourselves with family.'

'Plenty of people offered to come,' she said quickly. 'But this trip was something I needed to do alone.'

He said nothing, just looked at her with his warm, brown eyes.

'I wish I could have come with Mum before she died, though. She always hoped to return to Greece, with Dad and me, to show me her country, but sadly it never happened,' she found herself explaining, to fill the silence.

'Because of her MS?'

'Yes. Mostly.'

But even before her mother's diagnosis the

trip had been talked about but never actually planned. Her parents' restaurant had taken all their energy, money and time. At first it had seemed to be going from strength to strength, but then the unimaginable had happened. Dad had died and without him Mum had become a shadow of herself and had talked less and less about returning to Greece.

It had only been later that she'd realised that her father's death and struggling with a failing business hadn't been the only reasons Mum had been listless. She'd hidden her symptoms from her daughter until the evening she'd collapsed. And that had been the beginning of a new nightmare.

'What do you do when you're not working?' he asked, when she didn't expand.

'I kind of work all the time,' she admitted 'It's honestly my favourite thing to do.'

He frowned as if he didn't believe her. But it was true. She loved her work and found it totally absorbing. Given the choice of a night out or settling down to some research with a glass of wine in one hand, the research won hands down.

Their food arrived and was set before them. Katherine reached for the bowl of lemon quarters at the same as Alexander. As their fingers touched she felt a frisson of electricity course through her body. She drew back too quickly and flushed.

He lifted up the dish, his expression enigmatic. 'You first.'

'Thank you.'

'So why public health?' he asked, seeming genuinely interested.

'I thought I wanted to do general medicine but I spent six months in Infectious Diseases as part of my rotation and loved it—particularly when it came to diagnosing the more obscure infections. It was like solving a cryptic crossword puzzle. You had to work out what it could be by deciphering the clues, and that meant finding out as much as you could about your patient—where they, or their families, had been recently, for example. Sometimes it was obvious if they'd just come from Africa—then you'd start by think of malaria—or typhoid or if they'd been on a walking holiday in a place where there were lots of sheep, making Lyme disease a possibility. It was the patients who made the job so fascinating. When you'd found out as much as you could, you had to decide what tests and investigations to do, ruling diseases out one by one until the only one left was almost certainly the right answer.'

She rested her fork on the side of her plate.

'Of course, it wasn't always a good outcome. Sometimes by the time you found out what the patient had it was too late. And what was the point in diagnosing someone with malaria if you couldn't stop them getting it in the first place? I became really interested in prevention and that's when I moved into public health.' She stopped suddenly. 'Sorry. I didn't mean to go on. But when I get talking about work…'

'Hey, I'm a doctor, I like talking shop.'

'Why did you decide to come back to Greece?' she asked.

Something she couldn't read flickered behind his eyes. 'I wanted to spend more time with my daughter,' he said shortly. 'But we were talking about you. How did your parents meet?' It seemed he was equally determined to turn the conversation back to her.

'Mum met Dad when he was in the armed forces. He was stationed in Cyprus and she was visiting friends there. They fell in love and he left the army and they moved back to Scotland. He tried one job after another, trying to find something he enjoyed or at least was good at. Eventually he gave up trying to find the ideal job and started working for a building company. We weren't well off—not poor but not well off. We lived in a small house bordering an estate where there was a lot of crime. When I was eight my father became unwell. He didn't know what was it was—except that it was affecting his lungs. He was pretty bad before Mum persuaded him to see his GP.' She paused. 'That's when I began to think of becoming a doctor.'

He leaned forward. 'Go on.'

'We used to go, as a family, to his doctor's appointments. We did everything as a family.' Sadness washed over her. 'First there were the visits to the GP, but when he couldn't work out what was going on, he referred Dad to the hospital. I was fascinated. Everything about the hospital intrigued me: the way the doctors used to rush about seeming so important; the way the nurses always seemed to know what they were doing; the smells; the sounds—all the stuff that normally puts people off I found exciting.

'Of course, I was too young to understand that the reason we were there was because there was something seriously wrong with my father. His physician was a kind woman. I remember her well. She had these horn-rimmed glasses and she used to look at me over the top of them. When she saw how interested I was, she let me listen to my father's chest with her stethoscope. I remember hearing the dub-dub of his heartbeat and marvelling that this thing, this muscle, no larger than his fist, was what was keeping him—what was keeping me and everyone else—alive.

'I was always smart at school. It came easy to me to get top marks and when I saw how proud it made my parents, I worked even harder. My school teachers told my parents that they had high hopes for me. When I told Mum and Dad—I was twelve—that I wanted to be a doctor they were thrilled. But they knew that it would be difficult if I went to the high school in our area. It had a reputation for being rough and disruptive. They saved every penny they could so they could send me to private school.

'My father had received a payment from the building company when he left—by this time he'd been diagnosed with emphysema from years of breathing in building dust—but I knew he'd been planning to use the money for a down payment on a mortgage to buy a little restaurant—Dad would be the manager, Mum the head cook—and I didn't want them to use their life savings on me, not if they didn't have to.

'I persuaded them to let me apply to one of the top private schools. My teacher had told them that the school awarded scholarships to children with potential but not the funds to go to the school. She also warned them that it was very competitive. But I knew I could do it—and I did.'

'I am beginning to suspect that you're not in the habit of letting obstacles get in your way.'

Suddenly she was horrified. She wasn't usually so garrulous and certainly not when it came to talking about herself. Over the years she'd become adept at steering the conversation away from herself and onto the other person. Now she was acutely conscious of having monopolised the conversation, and when she thought about it she realised she'd made herself out to be a paragon of virtue when nothing could be further from the truth. Perhaps it was the wine. Or the way he listened to her as if she were the most fascinating person he'd ever met. Her heart thumped. Perhaps this was the way he was with everyone. She suspected it was. In which case he'd be an excellent family doctor.

'So how long have you been back in Greece?' she asked when their waiter left them, after replenishing their water glasses. She really wanted to know more about *him*.

'Just over two years.' His gaze dropped to his glass. He twirled his water, the ice cubes tinkling against the side. 'Not long after I lost my wife. I worked at St George's in London—As I mentioned earlier, I trained as surgeon before going into general practice—but my wife, Sophia, wasn't really a city girl, so we bought a house in a nearby suburb and I commuted from there. And when I was on call, I slept at the hospital.' A shadow crossed his face. 'In retrospect, that was a mistake,' he murmured, so softly she couldn't be sure she'd heard him correctly. 'Why did you change to general practice?'

His expression darkened. 'I gave surgery up when I decided to return to Greece.'

It wasn't really an answer and she had the distinct feeling he was keeping as much back from her as he was telling her. Had he really been content to give up the challenges and adrenaline rush of surgery to return to Greece to be a GP? But bereavement often caused people to change their lives.

'Was your wife Greek?'

'Yes.'

'Did she work while you were in the UK?' she asked. How had she felt about leaving her country and going to a much colder, much greyer London? But, then, she had been with the man she'd loved and who had loved her. No doubt she hadn't cared.

'She was a musician,' he replied. 'She always wanted to play in an orchestra. She gave that up when we moved to England and taught piano instead.'

'Crystal must miss her terribly.'

'We both do. I see her mother in Crystal every day.' He swallowed and averted his gaze from hers for a few moments. 'What about you?' he asked, eventually. 'Don't you want children?'

He was looking at her again with that same intense expression in his eyes.

'Don't most women? But…' She dropped her head and fiddled with her butter knife, searching for the right words. 'It wasn't meant to be,' she finished lamely. Her heart thumped uncomfortably against her ribs. *Keep the conversation on neutral territory,* she told herself. 'I enjoyed the trip to Olympia. You know a lot about Greek archaeology and history,' she said.

He slid her a thoughtful look as if he knew she was deliberately changing the subject.

'My father was an archaeologist and my wife shared his passion,' he said. 'What chance do you think I wouldn't be? I doubt there is an archaeological site in Greece I haven't been to. Every holiday, when we returned here, that's what we did. I think my wife thought it was her mission in life to educate me.' His face clouded and Katherine knew he was thinking of his wife again. He had loved her very much, that much was clear.

What would it be like—the thought almost came out of nowhere—to be loved like that? To know that there was one person in the world who treasured you above all else? That there was someone you could turn to in your darkest moments, share your deepest secrets and fears with?

It was unlikely she'd ever know.

Katherine sank back into the leather seat of her replacement car, grateful she didn't have to drive back to the villa on dark, twisting roads. Alexander switched on the radio, and the soothing notes of a Brahms concerto softly filled the silence that had sprung up between them since they'd left the restaurant. The lights of the dashboard and the occasional passing vehicle revealed a man absorbed with his own thoughts, his forehead knotted, his eyes bleak. He turned the volume up a little more.

'You like this?' she asked. 'It's one of my favourites.'

He glanced at her. 'It is? My wife used to play it all the time. I haven't listened to it for a while...' He looked away, his mouth set in a grim line.

His wife was like a ghostly presence in the car.

Katherine closed her eyes. Deliberately shifting her focus from Alexander, she wondered how Stéfan was faring. If it was meningitis, he could very well be struggling for his life at this moment. She hoped she was wrong and he just had an infection that would be quickly cleared up with antibiotics.

Becoming aware they had entered the village, she sat straighter in her seat.

Tension seeped between them as he brought the car to a standstill outside her villa. They unclipped their seat belts and climbed out of the car.

As he handed her the keys, their fingers touched. She looked up at him from beneath her lashes, wondering if he had felt the electricity too. Would he ask to come in? Or if he could see her again?

Instead, his voice was as neutral as his words. 'I enjoyed today. Thank you, Katherine.'

Disappointment washed over her. But what had she expected? It was clear he was still grieving for his wife.

'I did too. Good night…'

'Good night, Katherine.'

She winced inwardly as she heard the finality

in his tone. Hercules, purring loudly, curved his body around her legs as she opened the front door.

He was some comfort at least.

As the door closed behind her, Alexander thrust his hands deeper into his pockets and, before turning for the short walk home across the square, cursed himself for the fool he was.

Throughout the day he had been aware of the rising of desire he felt for this strait-laced, reserved, intelligent and beautiful woman. But hearing the melody Sophia had played so often had reminded him that Katherine would be leaving too. Even if she hadn't he had only ashes to give her.

No, his first instincts had been correct. It wouldn't be right to become entangled with this hurting woman.

CHAPTER THREE

'YIA-YIA SAYS you must come to our house.'

Katherine started. She hadn't been aware of Crystal coming in. Now here she was again, as bold as brass in her sitting room, as if she had every right to be there. But, then, Katherine conceded silently, she had extended what had amounted to an open invitation.

'Excuse me?'

'Yia-Yia says you helped Baba with his hand so she wants you to come to dinner. She says it's not good for someone to be alone all the time.'

'Yia-Yia? Your grandmother?' When Crystal nodded, she added, 'Does your father know you're here?'

The little girl hitched her shoulders and flopped her arms to her side, her hands bumping against her legs. 'I did tell him.' Her sigh was dramatic. 'He's working on his boat again. He also wants you to come.'

Katherine wasn't sure she believed Crystal.

She didn't want to impose herself on Alexander's family—particularly if he'd be there. He'd come to the villa the evening after they'd been to Olympia to tell her that her diagnosis had been correct. Stéfan did indeed have meningitis and was in Intensive Care. But Alexander hoped that, because of her alerting them to look out for meningitis, Stéfan would recover.

She hadn't seen Alexander since then but, to her dismay, she'd found herself thinking about him—a lot—during the week and knew she was in real danger of developing a crush on him. An unreciprocated crush, clearly, and someone like him was bound to pick up sooner or later the effect he was having on her. The ending of their evening together had indicated, more than words could, that he wasn't interested in pursuing a relationship with her. No, if the invitation had been extended by him, it had been out of politeness—from one colleague to another.

In which case it would be better not to encourage Crystal to visit too much.

Katherine managed a smile. 'I'm very busy, Crystal, so…' she picked up her pen pointedly '…would you thank your grandmother very much for her kind invitation but tell her I won't be able to make it?'

But instead of taking the hint, Crystal came

to stand next to her. 'What are you doing?' she asked.

'It's a paper I'd like to finish before I go back to work.'

'Like homework?'

'Exactly.' Trying to ignore the child next to her, Katherine made a few more notes on the page. But it was clear Crystal had no intention of leaving any time soon.

She suppressed a sigh and put her pen down. 'Would you like some orange juice?'

'Yes, please.'

When she got up to fetch it, both Hercules and Crystal followed her into the small kitchen.

'I told Baba that Yia-Yia and me thought you must be lonely all by yourself and he agreed. So it's good I can keep you company sometimes.'

As Katherine crouched down to give Hercules some food she felt her cheeks grow hot. It was bad enough, mortifying enough, that Alexander had said that, but for him, his six-year-old and his grandmother to be discussing her was too much. Was that what this dinner invitation was about? A let's-keep-the-solitary-woman-company-for-at-least-one-night-so-that-we-don't-have-to-worry-about-her-being-on-her-own? She swore silently.

It made it more important than ever that she

stay away from him; she absolutely refused to be the object of sympathy.

'You can tell your father, as I've already told him, I'm perfectly happy being on my own. I'm not in the least bit lonely.' Why was she justifying herself to a child? If she *did* feel a little bereft at times, it was only to be expected after losing Mum so recently. She handed Crystal the glass of juice.

'I could paint your toenails if you like,' Crystal said. She held up a plastic bag. 'Look, I got three different colours for my birthday from Cousin Helen. Baba says I'm too young to be wearing nail polish.' Her mouth drooped. 'Helen shouldn't have given it to me if I couldn't wear it. What was she thinking?'

The last phrase sounded so much like something her friend Sally would have said, it made Katherine smile.

'If you let me do your nails, it'll make you even more beautiful,' Crystal continued plaintively, and apparently without the tiniest hint of guile.

Katherine knew when she was beaten. 'Okay,' she said.

A smile of delight spread across Crystal's face. 'Can I? Really?'

'Yes, but *only* my toes. I don't wear varnish

on my fingernails. A doctor has to keep their fingernails short.' She held up her hands and wiggled them.

'Okay. You sit on the couch and put your feet on this chair,' Crystal instructed, lugging one of the kitchen chairs over.

Wondering whether she'd made a mistake by agreeing to the child's demands, Katherine slid her feet out of her sandals and placed them on the vinyl-covered seat. 'Like this?'

Crystal nodded. She opened the popper of her little plastic bag and very carefully placed three pots of nail varnish on the table. 'What colour would you like?'

Katherine studied the pots of varnish for a moment. One was deep purple and completely out of the question, even if she intended to re-move the polish at the first opportunity, the sec-ond was deep red and the third a pale, coral pink.

She pointed to the pink one. 'That one.'

'But I like the red.' Crystal pouted.

Katherine bit down on a smile. 'Okay. Red it is.'

She leaned against the back of the couch and closed her eyes. Crystal's little hands were like feathers on her feet and, to her surprise, Kath-erine found it very soothing.

'There. Done. Look!' Crystal said eventually. She stood back to admire her work. 'I told you it would be pretty.'

Katherine peered down at her toes. It was as if someone had taken a machete to them, lopping them off somewhere below the metatarsals. There had to more nail polish on her skin and the seat of the chair than on her nails. But Crystal looked so pleased with herself that Katherine quickly hid her dismay. 'Mmm. Quite a difference.'

Crystal tugged her hand. 'Come on, let's show Baba.'

'I don't think your father—'

But Crystal was pulling her to her feet. 'Helen wouldn't let me do hers, but when she sees yours, she will.'

'Crystal! I said ten minutes!' Alexander's voice came from below the balcony.

'Coming, Baba. In a minute.'

'Now, Crystal!'

Keeping her toes spread as far apart as possible, Katherine hobbled over to the balcony and looked down. Alexander was wiping grease-stained hands on a rag. His T-shirt clung damply to his chest and his hair was tousled. Yet he still managed to look like a Greek god.

'Hi, Katherine.' His teeth flashed. 'Sorry I'm

calling up, but my feet are sandy, my hands grubby and I need a dip in the sea before I'm fit for company. You are coming to dinner, aren't you?'

Crystal bumped against her as she climbed excitedly onto the rung of the balcony. 'She says not to dinner, Baba, but can she come for a visit? She is much more beautiful now! You have to see her.'

Katherine was about to protest when his eyes locked on hers. 'The part I can see of her already looks pretty good.' For a long moment the world seemed to disappear until there were just the two of them. 'Why not dinner?' he asked, breaking the spell.

'Because I've work to do and, anyway, I don't like to intrude on your family.'

'I assume you take time off to eat?'

'Yes, you have to eat!' his daughter echoed.

'My grandmother will be disappointed if you don't. She's already started preparing her best dishes.'

Alexander's family appeared determined to adopt her. She winced at her choice of words and sought desperately for an acceptable excuse. Apart from the effect Alexander had on her, every time she looked at Crystal she was painfully reminded of what she'd lost.

'Yes, *lahanodolmádes* and *patátes yemistés*,' Crystal added. 'Oh, and *baklavás* for afters! What else, Baba?'

'Crystal, could you please stop interrupting everyone?' He looked at Katherine again. 'Stay for dinner at least and then you can leave.'

It seemed that she had no choice but to allow herself to be dragged out of the house—it would be churlish to continue refusing not only Alexander's pleas but those of his daughter too. And to be honest, her mouth had started to water when Crystal had been listing the menu. It was a long time since she'd tasted home-cooked Greek food like her mother used to make.

'Yes, then. I'd love to.'

Crystal, victorious, clenched her fist and stabbed her folded elbow backwards. 'Yes-s-s! I'll see you at home, Baba. I'll bring her.'

'Not *her*, Crystal. Dr Burns.'

'Katherine is fine,' Katherine said.

He grinned at her. 'You did bring this on yourself, you know, by being so mysterious and elusive.'

Mysterious? Was that how he saw it? That she was the elusive one? She couldn't help smiling back.

'And you did tell Crystal she could visit. My daughter appears to find you irresistible.'

Her heart plummeted. She preferred *him* to find her irresistible.

The pint-sized tyrant wouldn't even let her stop to put on her sandals, saying severely that she would spoil it all if she tried to put them on too soon.

Alexander's home was set back from the village square and up a steep, narrow path. It was several times larger than hers, with shuttered windows, a cobbled driveway and paths and lush, established grounds. He must have a wonderful view from the wide balconies of his cliff-top home.

It took a while for Katherine's eyes to adjust to the dim interior after the bright light and blinding white beach outside. The house was cool, probably because it was shuttered against the heat of the day, although now the shutters were spread wide, allowing a breeze to penetrate the rooms. Despite Crystal hurrying her along, Katherine managed to catch glimpses of her surroundings: engraved, dark wood furniture; colourful striped rugs on polished terracotta tiles; and montages of family photographs, old and new, on white, rough-plastered walls. Crystal swept her into the kitchen where Katherine's senses were assailed with the aromas of garlic, herbs and browning meat.

A plump white-haired woman, bent over the pots steaming on an enormous traditional stove, lifted her head. She smiled warmly at Katherine and addressed her rapidly in Greek.

'Yia-Yia welcomes you and says she's happy you are here, visiting our home,' Crystal translated. 'Please sit at the table.' Without allowing Katherine time to reply, she turned to her grandmother and spoke in Greek, pointing excitedly to Katherine's toes. The older woman leant over and exclaimed. Katherine didn't need to understand any Greek to gather she was praising her great-granddaughter's efforts. Crystal's face said it all.

She had barely sat down before a plate of spanakopita was set down in front of her. Crystal's great-grandmother turned back to her stove, muttering happily.

'Aren't you glad you came?' Crystal said triumphantly. 'Look how pleased she is!'

If the child hadn't been so young, Katherine would have suspected her of engineering the whole situation.

'What's your great-grandmother's name?' Katherine asked.

'Yia-Yia, silly.'

Katherine took a bite of the miniature spinach and feta pie. She flapped a hand in front of her mouth. 'Hot. *Thermo.* Hot. But wonderful,' she added hastily. Two pairs of dark brown eyes studied her 'No, I mean what should *I* call her?'

'The same as everyone. Yia-Yia. She knows your name. Baba told her. I'm just going to get him!' Crystal said, flying out of the door.

Yia-Yia beckoned Katherine over to where she was working and pointed at the leaves of pastry she had laid out on a baking tray. She brought her fingers to her lips and made a smacking sound. It was clear she was showing Katherine what she was making for supper and that it would be delicious. Katherine could only smile and nod in response.

She was almost relieved when Crystal returned, dragging Alexander in her wake. His hair glistened almost black from his shower and he had changed into a bitter-chocolate T-shirt and cotton jeans. 'Show Baba your toes,' Crystal ordered.

Grimacing to herself, Katherine did as she was asked. She saw the leap of laughter in Alexander's eyes as he dutifully studied her feet. 'Very beautiful,' he said to Katherine, before murmuring so his daughter couldn't hear. 'Do you actually have toes at the ends of those feet? Or should I get the suture kit out again?'

Katherine spluttered with laughter, just managing to turn it into a cough at the last moment. But suddenly Alexander was whooping with laughter and she was too. She couldn't remember the last time she'd laughed like that. Yia-Yia and Crystal looked puzzled for a moment then they were whooping too, Yia-Yia's deep brown eyes almost disappearing in her chubby face.

'What's so funny?' Crystal asked, when everyone stopped laughing.

Alexander tweaked her nose. 'If you don't know, why did you join in?'

'I couldn't help it.' She was hopping from foot to foot. 'I just liked hearing you laugh, Baba.'

The atmosphere in the room changed subtly and the light in Alexander's eyes disappeared, replaced by something Katherine couldn't read.

'If you'll excuse me,' he apologised, 'a neighbour is complaining of a tight chest. It's nothing that staying off cigarettes wouldn't help, but his wife is always happier if I look in on him. I'll be back in a little while.' He turned to his grandmother and spoke to her. She nodded, unsmiling.

'Can I come, Baba?' his daughter asked.

'Of course. You know I always like to have my little helper with me. As long as you stay out of the way and as quiet as a mouse.' He caught Katherine's eye and raised an eyebrow.

'My daughter as quiet as a mouse? Who am I kidding?' he murmured, his lips curving into a smile.

Crystal was out of the door almost before he'd finished speaking.

Once again, Katherine was left alone with Yia-Yia. There was an awkward silence for a moment before the older woman beckoned Katherine to come forward. With a series of hand gestures and nods of the head, she indicated to Katherine that she wanted her help to finish preparing the meal.

'I'm sorry, I can't cook,' Katherine protested. There had never been a need to learn. When her mother had been alive and Katherine had been living at home they'd always eaten at the restaurant. And when she'd moved out and into her first flat she'd taken her main meal at the hospital or had eaten simple salads or pasta for supper. Then, when Mum had become too unwell to be on her own and Katherine had moved back home to look after her, she had fetched Greek delicacies from a nearby restaurant—their own having been sold a couple of years earlier—in an attempt to tempt Mum's failing appetite.

But almost before she'd finished speaking she was being passed a bowl of minced lamb and handed bunches of pungent-smelling herbs. Either Yia-Yia didn't understand what she was saying, or it had never crossed her mind that not all women liked cooking.

In the end it was one of the most peaceful and relaxing hours Katherine could remember spending for a long time. With Crystal's grandmother coaxing her along, while keeping a watchful eye on what she was doing, Katherine stuffed vine leaves and baked rich syrupy cakes. Every now and again the old woman would cluck her tongue and shake her head. At other times she'd nod, murmur something in Greek, and smile approvingly.

When dinner had been prepared to her satisfaction, and Alexander and Crystal still hadn't returned, Yia-Yia took her hand and led her outside to a bench in the garden. For the next ten minutes they sat in peaceful silence as the sun sank in the sky.

After a little while Yia-Yia gestured that they should go back inside. By the time Alexander and Crystal returned, a spread that could have fed eight had been laid out on the dining-room table.

Alexander's dark eyes swept over Katherine and he grinned, making her heart skip a beat. 'Somehow I never quite saw you as being domesticated,' he said.

Catching sight of her reflection in the large mirror on the wall, Katherine realised she was still wearing the flowery apron Grandmother had insisted she put on. Added to her bare feet and splotchy nail polish, she must look ridiculous. Her hair was a mess and clinging to her flushed cheeks. And was that a smudge of flour? Liking to appear neat and tidy at all times, tailored dresses with tights and decent shoes or smart trousers and blouses were what she usually wore. Two weeks in Greece and her colleagues would hardly recognise her. *She* barely recognised herself.

But, oddly, she rather liked the look of the woman in the mirror.

She seemed different from the last time he'd seen her, Alexander thought, studying Katherine from the corner of his eye. But if possible she was even more beautiful. Her blonde hair, bleached white-gold from the sun, had come loose from her plait and damp tendrils curled around her cheeks. A tiny wisp of hair clung to the corner of her mouth and he curled his hands inside the pockets of his jeans to stop himself from reaching out to tug it away. His grandmother's apron and the smudge of flour on her nose only added, somehow, to her allure. But those feet! As he'd said, it looked as if someone had bludgeoned her toes with a hammer.

It had been Yia-Yia and Crystal's idea to invite her for dinner. He'd tried to dissuade them, but his grandmother had insisted that not to, after Katherine had helped him, was not the Greek way. He'd had no choice but to agree. And, whatever he'd told himself, he was glad that she was here.

There was something about Katherine that drew him and despite everything he'd told himself he hadn't been able to stop thinking about her. He wasn't sure what to make of her. Her blue eyes were the colour of the sea at its deepest—more so when sadness overtook her. Was it only the loss of her mother that was causing that look in her eyes? She intrigued him. One minute she'd be the cool professional, like when they'd helped the young man who'd collapsed, the next she'd be blushing at something he'd said or refusing to hold his gaze, ill at ease in his company. And then over dinner she'd seemed to relax. At least until he'd asked her about her private life.

When Helen had found out they'd met and she'd sutured Alexander's hand and they'd spent the day together, her curiosity had known no bounds. That Katherine was also doctor tickled her.

'Perhaps she's like you,' she'd said. 'Maybe she has lost her lover and is here to mend her broken heart.' Helen liked to spin stories, usually romantic ones, about people. 'Yes, it has to be a broken love affair, I'm sure of it.' She'd slid him a mischievous look. 'Perhaps together you can mend your broken hearts.'

Despite himself, he'd laughed. 'You know I'm not interested in getting married again.'

'It's been two years, Alexander. A man like you isn't meant to be on his own. Grandmother won't be around for ever. I have my own life in Athens and as much as I love you both, I can't keep making trips down here every weekend, especially when it means leaving Nico on his own. And once we get married...' She shrugged. 'I won't be able to come so often. Crystal needs a mother. Someone who can be there for her all the time.'

'Crystal has me,' he'd replied tersely. 'No one can ever take Sophia's place.'

Helen was instantly contrite. 'Of course not.' Then she'd smiled again. It was hard for his cousin to stay serious for long. 'Anyway, who's saying anything about marriage?'

Typical Greek women. Always trying to matchmake.

'She is good at cooking,' his grandmother said to him in Greek, drawing him back to the present. 'For an Englishwoman. But she is too skinny. She should eat more.'

He grinned at the older woman. If she had her way they'd all eventually have to join a slimming club. 'I think she looks fine.'

'At least she dresses like a good Greek woman. No shorts up to her bottom like your cousin.'

Under the apron, Katherine was wearing a pair of light cotton trousers and a white blouse, neatly buttoned almost to the neck. No wonder his grandmother approved.

Katherine was looking at him enquiringly and he realised they had been speaking in Greek and excluding her.

'My grandmother says you are a good cook.'

'It's been fun—and informative,' Katherine admitted with a wry smile.

'But why does she seem so sad?' his grandmother continued. 'What does she have to be sad about? She is here in Greece, working in my kitchen, making food, and about to eat a fine meal.'

'Her mother died not so long ago,' he replied.

His grandmother's face softened in distress. She pulled Katherine into her arms and patted her on the back. 'Poor girl,' she said. A bewildered Katherine stared at him over her shoulder and he had to fight not to laugh.

He sobered. 'I told my grandmother that your mother died recently. She is saying she is sorry.'

Katherine gently extricated herself from his grandmother's arms. 'Tell her thank you, but I'm all right.'

'And what about a husband?' Yia-Yia continued. 'Where is he? Has she left him in England?' She clicked her tongue. 'A woman shouldn't leave her husband. Where is her ring?'

'She's not married, Grandmother.'

'And why not? She is old not to be married! Is she one of those modern women who think they don't need husbands? Or is she divorced?' Her mouth turned down at the corners. Grandmother didn't approve of divorce.

'I don't think she's ever been married, Yia-Yia.'

She looked relieved. 'Good. Perhaps she will fall in love with you. Would you like that? I think you like her, no?'

Katherine was watching him, waiting for him to translate, but he was damned if he was going to tell her how interested his grandmother was in her marital status—and her suitability as a partner for him.

'Grandmother is saying she is happy to have you here in her kitchen. She hopes you will come often.'

'Tell her it's lovely to be here.'

To his relief, the business of serving them all dinner prevented further comments from his grandmother. Crystal insisted on sitting next to Katherine, her body pressed so tightly against her Katherine had to find it difficult to eat. Yet she said nothing. She laid down her knife so that she could eat with one hand. Crystal was a friendly child but he'd never known her to form an attachment quite as quickly. It wasn't as if she wasn't surrounded by love.

'So you don't work on weekends?' Katherine asked him. They had taken their coffee onto the balcony. She'd offered to help clear away but his grandmother wouldn't hear of it, insisting it was Crystal's job. Or at least that was what Alexander had told Katherine. Grandmother would have been only too delighted to keep their guest in her kitchen while she cooked some more.

'Carlos—my partner, who you met briefly— and I take turns and we have a colleague who fills in the rest of the time. He retired early so he could spend more time on his thirty-footer, but he likes to keep his hand in.'

'What news about Stéfan?'

'He's still in Intensive Care.'

'But he is going to be okay?'

'I don't know.' He rubbed the back of his neck. 'He's on a ventilator. They think it's a rare type of bacterial meningitis that he has. They're still doing tests.' He stood. 'I'm sorry, but you're going to have to excuse me. It's time for Crystal's bedtime and she likes me to read her a story.'

'Of course. I should get back anyway and do some more work before I turn in.' Her cheeks had flushed. 'Please say good night to Crystal and thank your grandmother for me. I had very pleasant evening.'

'You'll come again?' he asked. She was easy company and he found being with her restful. Actually, who was he kidding? He just liked being with her.

'I don't want to keep intruding,' she said, the colour in her cheeks deepening.

'You're not. Trust me.'

She gave him the ghost of a smile and left.

He watched her pick her way down the steps and into the square. He'd found it difficult to concentrate on his paperwork the last few days.

His thoughts kept straying back to her, distracting him. Yes, he thought. She was a distraction—a very enjoyable one—but that was all she would ever be.

CHAPTER FOUR

THE FOLLOWING MORNING, just after dawn had lightened the sky and Katherine had taken her coffee out to the balcony, she noticed that Alexander was back working on his boat. In which case she would work inside, at least until she was sure he'd gone. She'd already had more to do with him than was wise. Relationships, particularly brief flings with attractive Greek doctors still grieving for their wives, had no place on her agenda.

But even as she reminded herself of that, she wondered if she could make an exception. It would be so good to feel someone's arms around her again. Good to have company, good to have someone to share walks and trips with, and who better than a man she would never see again once she'd left here?

She shook her head to chase the thoughts away. She suspected he found her attractive, but that wasn't the same thing as wanting even a casual relationship with her. And just how casual did she want it to be? Unbidden, she imagined him naked, tanned body against white sheets, his hands exploring every inch of her.

She retreated back inside and determinedly fired up her computer. Work. That was what kept her sane. Her paper was what she should be concentrating on.

She edited all day, acutely aware that her attention kept wandering back to Alexander. Just before supper she heard the excited voice of Crystal and, unable to resist a peek, peered out at the bay. He was there again, but this time in the water with his daughter.

She watched as he raised Crystal above his head before tossing her in the air and catching her just before she hit the water. The little girl shrieked with pleasure and wrapped her arms around her father's neck. A few minutes later Alexander, Crystal balanced on his shoulders, waded out of the water, his swimming shorts clinging to narrow hips and lean but muscular thighs.

It wasn't just that she found him sexy as hell. She liked the way he was with his child—clearly she was the centre of his universe and that was the way it should be: a child's happiness should always be paramount. Her chest tightened. What would he think if he knew her secret? Not that she was ever to going to share it with him.

She went into the kitchen and made herself a Greek salad with some of local goat cheese and olives, along with plump, ripe tomatoes she'd bought from the village store. Telling herself it was far too beautiful an evening to eat inside, she took her plate out to the lower veranda. Alexander and Crystal had disappeared, no doubt having gone home to have their evening meal. As the sun sank below the horizon, she sighed. Despite everything she'd told herself, their absence made her feel lonelier than ever.

Alexander excused himself from the game of cards he had been playing and, taking his beer, walked over to the small wall surrounding the village square. Crystal was riding her bike around the fountain in the centre in hot pursuit of the neighbour's boy, her little legs pedalling as fast as they could so she could catch up with him.

Alexander smiled as he watched her. He'd made the right decision, coming back. Crystal was thriving, his grandmother was delighted to have her close by and he was…well, content. As long as his daughter was happy he was too—or as much as he had any right to expect. Sometimes he wondered whether Crystal even remembered Sophia. She spoke of her mother periodically, asking if she were still in heaven and telling him that she knew Mama was watching her from the sky. Occasionally he would show Crystal video footage he'd taken of them on the too-rare occasions he'd taken leave and they'd come here. His daughter would lean forward and watch with shining eyes.

What would Sophia think if she knew he was back in Greece? How would she feel about him giving up his job in London? Would she be pleased that he'd finally, even when it was too late, realised what was important? Would she approve of the way he was bringing up their child? God, he still missed her and, God, he still felt so damned guilty.

He sipped his cold beer and gazed out over the sea. It was then he noticed Katherine. She'd just emerged from the water, her long legs emphasised by the black one-piece costume she was wearing. She dried off then wrapped the towel around her and sat with her back to him, knees pulled up to her chest, staring out at the same sea he was.

Under her prim exterior and natural reserve, there was a loneliness, an aura of something so vulnerable about her he found himself, for the first time since Sophia's death, wanting to know another woman better. But what did he have to offer? He wouldn't, couldn't, get married again. No one could ever match up to Sophia.

He took another gulp of his drink and turned away. Why had the possibility of getting married again even crossed his mind? The moonlight was making him fanciful. His life was complicated—and full—enough.

Crystal whizzed by him on her bike and waved. Right there was everything that mattered. He glanced at his watch. It was time to get his daughter to bed.

CHAPTER FIVE

As HAD BECOME a habit, Katherine was sitting outside his house on the bench with Grandmother, after spending a couple of hours cooking with her in the kitchen. She'd closed her eyes to savour the sensation of the breeze on her face, but when Grandmother poked her in her ribs with her elbow she opened them to see that Alexander was coming across the square towards them.

Katherine's heart leaped. Frightened of what he would read in her eyes, she lowered her lids until she was sure she could look at him calmly. She could deal with her developing crush on him as long as he never suspected.

'Hello, you two.' He bent and kissed his grandmother on her cheek and said something to her in Greek that made her laugh. Although Katherine's Greek was improving, when the Greeks spoke to each other it was usually too fast for her to follow.

Alexander grinned at Katherine. 'I've just asked her what she's thinking of, sitting down when dinner's due. She says now she has you to help her, sometimes she can take time off to enjoy the Greek sunshine.'

Nevertheless, the old woman got to her feet and retreated back inside, leaving her space on the bench for Alexander. He took a seat next to Katherine and, like she'd been doing earlier, turned his face up to the sun and closed his eyes. 'My grandmother is right. We all need to sit in the sun more often,' he murmured.

His usual vitality seemed to have deserted him and he looked tired.

'Is everything all right?' she asked.

'No, not really. Stéfan—the man with meningitis—died last night.'

'I'm so sorry. I really hoped he would be okay.'

He opened his eyes and turned to face Katherine. 'So did I, but once he developed multiorgan failure...' He paused. 'We've asked for a post-mortem but, according to the pathologist, it might be another week before they can do it. They have a bit of a backlog as his colleague is off on leave.' He rubbed the back of his neck and frowned. 'I was speaking to one of my colleagues in the area today and he tells me he's had a case too—a couple of days ago, a teenager. He's been admitted to a hospital in Athens.'

Katherine's antenna went on red alert. 'Two cases in a week? Doesn't that strike you as odd?'

'He isn't sure his patient has meningitis. He's going to call me as soon as he has the results of the lumbar puncture. But I'd be surprised if they both have it. As far as I'm aware, meningitis normally affects similar age groups.'

'Usually, but not always. It depends on the strain.'

'We'll find out soon enough. They're giving his patient's family antibiotics prophylactically to be on the safe side.'

'Sensible,' Katherine murmured. However, if Alexander's colleague's patient did turn out to have meningitis, it could be the start of something. Something terrifying.

'Any others you're aware of?' she asked.

'I rang around a few of the practices in the area, but no one else has come across any. I've told them to let me know if they do. I'm hoping these two will turn out to be random, unrelated events—supposing David, the teenage boy, does have it and, as I said, that isn't at all certain.'

He could be right, but there was a way she could find out.

She heard Grandmother calling Alexander from inside and got to her feet. 'Sounds like you're wanted.'

'I thought you'd want to know about Stéfan,' he said, rising too 'After I check in with Yia-Yia, I'm going to see the family of one of my other patients who I admitted to hospital after I diagnosed her with a nasty chest infection.' He smiled wryly. 'It's one of the privileges, but also one of the responsibilities, of being in general practice in Greece. Any member of a family becomes unwell and the rest expect you to see them through it as well. And that usually involves late-night tea and cakes and much discussion.'

Although she was disappointed he was going, the care he took of his patients was one of the things she liked about him. Besides, she wanted to do some checking up of her own.

She hurried back to her house. It was after six in the UK but Tim was divorced and rarely left work until much later.

She dialled the number of the office and was pleased when he picked up straight away. After exchanging small talk for a few moments—yes, she was enjoying her break and, yes, she would be coming back to work as planned at the end of September—she repeated what Alexander had told her.

'I've got a feeling about this,' she said. 'Is there any chance you could speak to your opposite number in Athens and ask him if there have been any more cases reported? I realise I'm probably being over-cautious but it wouldn't hurt to find out.'

'I doubt there will be anyone still there at this time. Will the morning do?'

'It will have to. As I said, it's probably nothing but it's best to be on the safe side. Thanks, Tim.'

He called her back on her mobile just before nine the next morning and came straight to the point.

'You were right,' he said. 'I've spoken to my opposite number in Athens and he tells me there have been reports of ten cases in and around the southern Peloponnese, including the two you mentioned. One or two would mean nothing but ten! It certainly suggests there is something to be concerned about.'

Excitement surged through Katherine. Her instinct had been right! 'What ages?'

'It varies. From teenagers to young adults. As you'd expect, it is the youngest who are most seriously affected. One child—a lad of seventeen—is in Intensive Care in Athens and it's not looking good.'

'The boy in Intensive Care—what's his name?'

'David Panagaris.'

Was he the same lad Alexander had told her about? It seemed likely. Her heart was racing. This is what she was trained to do. 'I could look into it. Could you let the department in Athens know I'm here and would like to help?'

'Absolutely not,' Tim protested. 'You're on holiday. They must have someone local they can call on. It's not as if Greece doesn't have public health doctors of their own.'

'Of course they do, but I happen to be here and I'm an expert in the spread of infectious diseases. I'm probably the most up-to-date person in Europe at the moment and you and I both know it's all much more co-operative now than it used to be. Come on, Tim, you know it makes sense.'

There was a long pause at the end of the phone. 'I guess it does makes sense,' Tim said reluctantly. 'But is your Greek good enough to ensure you ask the right questions and, more importantly, get the right answers?'

It wasn't. But Alexander's was. 'What about the Greek doctor I mentioned? The one who alerted me to the possibility of an outbreak? If he's prepared to take time out to help me, that would solve the problem of my not being fluent in Greek.' She wasn't really sure she wanted to work with Alexander. It was bad enough catching tantalising glimpses of him most days, without being thrust into his company all the time. But she wanted to do this and she couldn't without Alexander's help. 'I'll need to ask him, of course, but I've no doubt he'll say yes.'

'Okay,' Tim conceded. 'I'll suggest it to my colleague.' Katherine released a breath. 'What more info do you have?'

'In addition to the boy admitted to Intensive Care in Athens, there have been two deaths over the last ten days—your man and a woman tourist from France in her teens. Her family have already repatriated her body. No obvious links between the deceased as yet.'

Her excitement drained away. Three families had lost a loved one or were in danger of doing so. And if there was an epidemic, and there seemed little doubt that was what they could be dealing with, if they didn't locate all those who had come into contact with the sufferers and treat them, more people could die. In addition, they needed to find out where it was coming from so they could reach people before they became unwell.

'Could you give me the names and addresses of the patients? Plus the names of their family doctors, or the doctors who treated them?'

'I'll email them to you straight away.'

As soon as she disconnected, she phoned Alexander's surgery only to discover he wasn't expected in until later. She flung on some clothes and, without stopping for breakfast, set off across the square to Alexander's home, praying he'd be there and not out on a visit.

The sun was already blazing down and she was perspiring by the time she reached his door. She found Grandmother in the kitchen, making bread.

'Morning,' Katherine said in Greek. 'I need to speak to Alexander. Is he here?' She didn't have time for the usual pleasantries today.

Alexander's grandmother frowned, wiped her hands on a tea towel and shook her head. '*Nè*. At work.'

'Hello.' It was Crystal, looking sleepy in pyjamas and holding a teddy bear. She said something to her grandmother in Greek and went to stand next to Katherine, slipping her hand into hers. 'Yia-Yia says you're looking for Baba. She says he's gone to his consulting room in the village.' Grandmother had lifted a pot of tea and was holding it up. 'She wants to know if you'd like some tea. And some breakfast? She's just made some.'

'Please thank her for me and say I'd love to stay but I really need to see your father. It's urgent.'

The child relayed it back to to her grandmother, who looked disappointed she'd have no one to feed.

'Is something the matter?' Crystal asked.

'No.' Katherine crouched down and ruffled Crystal's hair. 'At least, nothing for you to worry about. I promise.'

Leaving the house, she headed back down the flight of steps and along the street to the rooms Alexander used as a surgery for the locals.

She tapped on the door of Alex's room and, without waiting for a reply, let herself in. He was sitting at the desk, his chair turned to face the window so that he had his back to her. He swivelled around to face her.

'I'm sorry,' he said. 'This isn't a good time.'

'I heard,' she said softly.

He frowned. 'Heard what?'

'About David Panagaris, that is the name of your colleague's patient, isn't it?' When Alexander nodded, she continued. 'I thought it must be him. I gather he's in Intensive Care. I'm sorry.'

Without waiting to be asked, she took the seat opposite him.

'Poor bloody parents. Perhaps if they'd brought him in sooner—' He broke off. 'How did you know he'd deteriorated? He was only admitted to Intensive Care last night.'

'My boss phoned me—I phoned him first. Let me explain.'

Alexander said nothing but leaned forward, placing his folded hands on the desk. He looked even more bushed than he had yesterday. There were dark circles under his eyes and underneath the tan he was drawn and pale. She wondered if he'd been up all night.

'As you know, my thesis for my doctorate is on meningitis and other bacterial infections—its spread and containment. That sort of thing. Our unit is one of the biggest in Europe but we have strong ties with others units across the world. We share information on all matters of public health, especially on infectious diseases. Over the last few years increasing numbers of countries across the world have bought into this collaborative approach. It makes sense to pool our resources rather than compete with one another. Africa, for example, has much better information on the spread of malaria, and so on…'

He nodded impatiently.

'When you told me about your cases it rang alarm bells so I phoned my boss and asked him to contact the public health department in Athens. Apparently, apart from Stéfan and David, there have been eight other cases all in, or around, this area, including another death—a young French girl' She held out her phone. 'My boss has emailed me a list with all their names.'

'Eight other cases?' Alexander looked instantly alert, all traces of his earlier tiredness having disappeared. 'So there is an epidemic?'

'It appears so. The thing is, I've offered to take the lead in looking into the situation. But I'm going to need help. My Greek isn't good enough for me to do it on my own.'

He narrowed his eyes. 'You want me to help?'

'Yes,' she said simply.

'Of course,' he said with no hesitation. 'I'll need to arrange for Dr Kanavakis—my retired colleague—to cover for me, but I don't think that will be a problem. When do we start?'

'Now.'

He raised his eyebrows. 'Let me make that phone call, then.'

When he'd finished he turned back to Katherine. 'Cover's sorted. Now, what else do you know about the cases?'

'Very little. I have the names and addresses of

all the patients. Most live in the southern part of Greece. Two come from Nafplio or very nearby. The French girl was on holiday there.'

He leaned back in his chair. 'Hell, that isn't good. A lot of cruise ships come into Nafplio. That will make tracing contacts more difficult.'

She checked the names on her phone. While Alexander had been on the phone she'd downloaded them into a document. 'What else can you tell me about David?'

'His parents live in a village close to Messini. He'd been snuffly and lethargic for most of the morning. They thought it was a cold, but when he deteriorated they brought him in to see my colleague. Unfortunately, he was already showing signs of septicaemia. He was given intravenous antibiotics and they arranged for an immediate transfer to hospital, but he was already in a bad way.' He raked a hand through his hair. 'He's only young.'

He jumped up and started pacing. 'If we do have an epidemic on our hands, none of the children will be safe.' He stopped in front of her. 'Come on. Let's go to the hospital. I'll let his doctor know what's happening. We need to find where the victims have been and who they've been in contact with.' He paused. 'Unless we should split up? You go to see the relatives of the other cases while I go to the hospital?'

'No,' she said, putting her hand on his arm. 'As I said, I might be the expert and know the questions to ask, but you can speak Greek and you're a local doctor. They'll find it more comfortable to talk to you and they might tell you things they wouldn't tell me. You'll also be able to pick up better than I if they are leaving out information that might be important. But what we should do is make sure the health services in Athens have put all the local family practices on alert, as well as warning the general public. Doctors and parents are more likely to be vigilant if they know what to look out for.'

'I'll speak to them, of course. What is the name of your contact there?'

Even before he put the phone down she could see the conversation hadn't gone the way he wanted. His voice had risen towards the end and he appeared to be arguing with whoever was on the other end. A muscle twitched in his cheek.

'They say they've warned the hospitals and practices to watch out for cases of meningitis but they won't put out a full alert on the radio or in the press. They say that if they do, people will panic and rush to the hospitals. They say the medical services will collapse under the strain and it's too early to take the risk.'

'I could phone my boss and get him to put pressure on them,' Katherine suggested. 'Although I suspect they'd do the same in the UK.'

'Be my guest.' He gestured to the phone. 'I doubt it would do any good. They're unlikely to do anything more until there are more cases. They insist the ones we know about might just be random at the moment—a blip, not connected at all.'

'It is possible,' Katherine said thoughtfully. 'We've noted and recorded many cases of infectious diseases in the past that seemed to be part of an epidemic but that turned out not to be. I think we should talk to the Stéfan's parents before we do anything else. As soon as I get the French girl's parents' contact details I'll call them.'

'Fine with me,' he said, picking up his medical bag. 'And I hope to God you're right about these cases not being connected. Stéfan's family is from a village near Sparta. We could go to the hospital in Athens from there.' He took his mobile from his pocket. 'I'll phone Carlos and let him know what's happening.'

The road leading to Sparta was the worst Katherine had ever been on. Travelling through and over the mountains, it was narrow, with barely enough room for two cars to pass safely. In addition, every few miles the road almost spun back on itself through a number of hairpin bends. She could barely bring herself to look. On her side of the car, the road fell away sharply and there were no road barriers to prevent the car, should it have to swerve to avoid oncoming vehicles, toppling over the side. Incredibly, the road conditions didn't stop drivers from overtaking, whether they could see or not.

'What's Crystal up to today?' she asked, trying to unclench her fists.

'She's having a sleepover with a friend a little way up the coast. Her friend's mother is coming to fetch her.'

'Could you slow down?' Katherine yelped, after they took a particularly sharp bend that she'd thought they'd never make.

Alexander turned to face her and grinned.

'If I slow down, it will only encourage other drivers to try and overtake us. They don't care whether the road is empty or not.'

'Please keep your eyes on the road at least.'

Despite her terror and worry about what they would be facing soon, she couldn't help admire the scenery as they whizzed along. Little villages clung to the side of the mountain, the houses often appearing to spill almost onto the road. Small cafés with old men outside, puffing on pipes or playing board games flew by in a blur. To her consternation, Alexander would often take his hand off the steering-wheel to give them a friendly wave as they passed.

At other times, almost out of nowhere, they'd come upon small farm stalls selling flowers or tomatoes or other freshly grown produce from the roadside. At any other time she might have enjoyed the trip and promised herself that once this emergency was over she'd come back—with her own car, of course—and savour the journey.

As she relaxed a little, her thoughts returned to the task in hand. She unfolded the map she'd brought with her and circled each victim's location with her pen. All of them lived in the Peloponnese, apart from the French girl, who had been on holiday there. Nevertheless, it was still a huge area.

'Is there any facility or event you know of that links the victims?' she asked Alexander.

He waited until he'd slowed down to let an overtaking car coming in the opposite direction pass before he spoke. 'None that I can think of. I'd have to study the map. I don't really keep on top of social events these days.'

A short time later, to Katherine's relief, they

turned off the mountain road and towards Sparta and the road became wider and straighter.

'The village is about thirty kilometres northwest of Sparta,' Alexander said. 'We should be there in about twenty minutes.'

Katherine's stomach churned. In a short while she'd be facing two very recently bereaved parents and she wasn't looking forward to it.

'What's Sparta like?' she asked, more to distract herself than out of any burning interest.

'Little of the original city remains. Most of the what you'll see as we pass through has been built on top of ancient Sparta.' He glanced at her. 'You know the stories of the Spartans?'

'Only that they were tough and didn't believe in creature comforts.'

'It's grimmer than that. Under a system known as the *agoge* Spartan boys were trained to be as physically tough as possible. They were taken from their families at the age of seven and made to live in barracks. They were deliberately underfed so they'd become adept at living off the land. The boy babies who weren't expected to make the grade were taken to the top of the mountain and left there to die.'

Katherine shuddered. 'Their poor mothers.'

'It was cruel. I can't imagine how they felt, having their sons ripped from their arms. I suspect some ran away with them, even though they risked death to save them.' He blinked. 'It's what Sophia would have done. She'd never let anything part her from her child.'

Katherine's heart lurched. What would he think if he knew what she'd done? She was glad he would never know.

'You should try to visit Mycenae, though,' he continued, apparently unaware of her reaction. 'It's almost intact. It's very close to Sparta— only a few kilometres at the most. It has a less bloody past.'

'Have you been there?' Her throat was so tight she could barely speak.

He glanced at her and smiled. 'Naturally.'

They turned off onto a minor road and continued. It was much flatter here, the land planted with olive trees and vines. But then they turned a corner, drove up a street so narrow it would be impossible for another car to pass, and into a small village square.

Now they were here, her anxiety about facing the bereaved parents returned.

'Are you all right about doing this?' Alexander asked.

'Yes.' She would be. She had to think of the children whose lives they would save rather than the one who was lost.

They parked the car and asked directions from an older man sweeping the square. He laid aside his brush and gestured for them to follow him. It was just as well because although the village was small, it was unlikely they would have found their way to the house, tucked away as it was behind a crumbling wall and almost hidden down one of the maze-like streets.

The house itself, like many of the others in the village, seemed to be built into the rock face.

A woman in a navy-blue long-sleeved dress answered their knock and after Alexander explained who they were, stepped aside to let them in.

Stéfan's parents were sitting in a darkened room surrounded by family and friends. They clung to each other and Katherine winced at the grief she saw etched on their faces.

This, she thought, was why she was an academic. Facing other people's pain, when she found it impossible to deal with her own, was something she'd spent most of her adult life trying to avoid. But she couldn't afford to be squeamish—or the luxury of dwelling on her own discomfort. However much she hated to intrude on their grief, she knew it was necessary.

Alexander introduced them againand very gently explained why they were there. 'I know this is a very difficult time for you, but we need to ask you some questions.'

Mr Popalopadous nodded. His wife seemed incapable of speaking. 'Please,' he said, 'ask your questions. If we can stop this happening to someone else's child…'

Katherine sat down and took Mrs Popalopadous's hands in hers. 'We need to know Stéfan's last movements—where he'd been before he became unwell and who he'd been in contact with.'

She looked bewildered. 'He was a teacher in the local school, but during the holidays he takes—took his boat out or went to the taverna with his friends. None of them are sick.'

Katherine exchanged a look with Alexander. None of them were sick *yet*.

'Should we quarantine the village?' Alexander murmured to her.

She shook her head slightly. 'Not yet.' She knew there was no point in getting ahead of themselves. What they had to do was retrace Stéfan's movements going back at least a week to establish who had come into contact with him. After that they needed to get in touch with those people where possible and make sure they—and anyone who had spent more than a few hours in their company—were given antibiotics.

When Mrs Popalopadous started sobbing

again, Katherine leaned forward. 'I know it's difficult, but can you think of anyone apart from his friends or his pupils he might have been in contact with?' She ignored the warning look Alexander gave her. She wasn't unsympathetic to Mrs Popalopadous's grief but what mattered most now was that no one else would die.

Mr Popalopadous answered for his wife. 'No. No one different.' He wrapped his arm around his wife's shoulders. 'Now, I'm afraid you must leave us. We have arrangements to make.'

His dignity in the face of his grief was humbling. But Katherine wanted to press him further. However, Alexander got to his feet and taking her by the elbow forced her to rise to hers too. He scribbled something on a piece of paper and handed it to the bereaved father. saying something in Greek Katherine couldn't follow.

His hand still on her elbow, Alexander ushered Katherine out of the house and to his car.

'I still had questions for them,' she protested.

'For God's sake, Katherine, they've just lost their child. They've told us all they can.

'You can't be sure of that. It's the things they don't think that are important that might matter most.'

'I gave him my mobile number and asked him

to call me, day or night, if anything else does come to mind. I also told them to go to their family doctor and make sure they, and anyone else who might have been in contact with Sté-fan, gets antibiotics. I'll call the family doctor to make sure they do—although I'm sure he'll have it in hand,'

'It won't hurt to make sure.' Katherine replied.

After he'd made the call, Alexander turned to her. 'As I thought, he plans to see them later this afternoon. As you can imagine, he's pretty keen that we get on top of this.' He frowned. 'The most likely source of the infection is the high school.'

'But not the only possibility!'

'No, but isn't it better to go with the most likely and work our way out from there?'

He did have a point. 'Perhaps once we've interviewed the other families something will jump out. In the meantime, I'd better get onto my boss and tell him to make double sure that all the medical facilities in the area are on red alert.'

'Shouldn't we do that?' Alexander asked.

'It's more important that we try and locate the source of the outbreak. My boss will liaise with your public heath team in Athens, although we should probably introduce ourselves at some point.'

They got into the car and Alexander turned the key in the ignition. 'Okay. Next stop Athens.'

'How long will it take us to get there?'

'About two and half hours. Less if you stop interfering in the way I drive.'

Katherine gritted her teeth. 'Just get there as soon as you can.'

Happily, it was a far better road to Athens than the one they'd come on. While they were driving, Katherine phoned the French girl's parents. Luckily her French was considerably better than her Greek. But that didn't make the conversation any less painful. Claire's father held himself together long enough to tell Katherine that Claire had been on a short break with her boyfriend in Greece when she'd become unwell. It had all been very sudden—too sudden for the family to make it to her bedside in time. There had been a long pause in the conversation when Claire's father had lost control, but eventually he had, for long enough at any rate to tell her that their family doctor had treated the family and the boyfriend with antibiotics.

Katherine repeated what she'd learned to Alexander and they'd sat in silence, each absorbed with their own thoughts. She wondered if Alexander was thinking, like she was, how devastating it was to lose someone you loved—especially when that person was young—like Claire—or Sophia. When, a while later, Katherine's stomach growled she realised she hadn't eaten since breakfast and Alexander would be in the same position.

'I don't know about you but I'm starving,' she admitted.

'Would you like to stop at one of the tavernas?' he asked.

'I'd prefer not to take too long over lunch. I'm keen to talk to David's family.'

'I know a place near here that does pastries and decent coffee. We could pick something up and get back on our way.'

She was pleased he was in just as much of a hurry to get to the hospital as she was. She didn't think she could have beared to have stopped at a café and had a proper lunch, especially when she'd learned that in Greece there was no such thing as fast food served in a restaurant. While most times she appreciated the care they put into their cooking, today wasn't one of them.

When they stopped, she bought some bread

rolls and cheese while Alexander downed a couple of cups of espresso in quick succession. She didn't care for the heavy, thick Greek coffee so she bought some fresh orange juice to go with their picnic lunch instead.

She took a few moments to split open the rolls and fill them. Alexander pulled a penknife from his pocket and offered it to her, and she quickly sliced the tomatoes and added them to the cheese. Once she'd done that she handed one of the rolls to Alexander. When she next looked up it was gone. He had to have wolfed it down in a couple of bites.

'Should I get some more?' she asked, astonished.

'No, that will do me for the time being. Shall we get on?'

She wrapped her half-eaten sandwich in a napkin. 'Suits me. I can finish this in the car.'

After they'd been driving for a while she asked, 'How long before we get there?'

He glanced at his watch. 'Another hour.'

She did some calculations in her head. An hour to get there, a couple more at the hospital and then what? A three or a three-and-a-half-hour journey back. They'd be lucky to reach home before midnight and they still had the other families to see.

However, it seemed he was there before her. 'I phoned a colleague while you were in the ladies. He's agreed to contact the doctors on our list and ask the families some preliminary questions. He said he'd call me back as soon as he had some information for us.'

Although Katherine would have preferred to have made the calls herself, she knew that Alexander had made the right decision. Every minute could make a difference—a life-changing difference—for one patient and his, or her, family.

Finally they arrived in Athens. After the peace of the countryside Katherine found the noise of tooting horns and the fumes of the cars that crept along the roads nose to tail almost overwhelming. She craned her neck to see the Acropolis, which dominated the city. It was on her list of places to visit but, like the rest of her plans, it would have to wait.

She was glad Alexander was with her to negotiate his way around the hospital. Although her spoken Greek wasn't too bad now, reading it was a completely different matter and despite many of the signposts being in English, it was still a busy and confusing hospital.

They made their way to the intensive care unit and she listened as Alexander explained to the doctor why they were there. Then he asked for an update on the patient.

'David is holding his own,' he said. 'But the septicaemia means we might have to amputate his hand. We have a theatre on standby.'

Oh, no! The boy was so young to be facing such drastic surgery. His parents must be beside themselves. And indeed, it seemed that they were too distraught to speak to them. The doctor apologised and suggested they come back in the morning when David's condition might have stabilised and the parents be more willing to see them.

'It can't wait,' Katherine protested. 'We have to find out where he's been and who he came into contact with. His family are the only people who can tell us.'

Once more, Alexander took her by the arm and led her away and out of earshot of the doctor.

'For God's sake, Katherine. Their child may be about to go into Theatre. Could you talk to anyone if you were in their position? I'm not sure I could.'

She knew why he was saying that, but she also knew that in circumstances such as these they couldn't afford the luxury of waiting.

'I know it's a bad time, but we need information as quickly as possible.'

'It can wait.'

'No, it can't.' She held his gaze. 'No it can't,' she repeated more softly. 'If you won't talk to them, I'll have to.'

He rubbed a hand across the back of his neck in what, she was beginning to realise, was a habit of his when he was thinking.

'Look, why don't I try to find another, less distressed family member to talk to? There's bound to be at least one here at the hospital—if I'm not mistaken most of the extended family will have gathered by now.'

'Fair enough,' Katherine conceded. 'But if they can't help I'm going to have to insist on speaking to David's parents.'

He nodded and Katherine was left kicking her heels while Alexander went in search of the extended family. While she waited she opened up her laptop and started creating a database. Then she reviewed what they'd learned so far— which wasn't much. They still didn't know what the cases had in common or how they might have come into contact with the virus. It was almost two hours before Alexander reappeared. He looked tired and in need of a shave.

'They decided they had to take David to Theatre and they've just taken him through to Recovery. They had to amputate the fingers on his left hand. Thank God he's right-handed.'

'I'm sorry,' she said. 'But it could have been so much worse.' She waited a few moments. 'Did you find out anything that might help?'

'Not really. I found his aunt, who lives next door to her sister. According to her, apart from school, a party and a trip to the beach he's not been anywhere out of the usual.' He held out a piece of paper. 'She's given me the names of the other kids at the party. None of them are the other victims, though.'

'They might be yet,' she said. 'We need to make sure everyone on that list and their doctors are contacted.'

'I telephoned Diane while I was waiting to hear how David got on in Theatre. She promised to get onto it straight away.'

She was impressed. She'd been right. Alexander was the perfect person to help with the crises.

'What about the other GP? The one you called—has he got back to you?'

'He phoned a few minutes ago. He's spoken to all the doctors, who have agreed to do as we requested.'

Alexander stepped forward and brushed a

lock of her hair away from her forehead. The unexpected and tender gesture made her heart tighten. 'We've done all we can for the moment,' he said gently. 'Let's go home. We can discuss what we're going to do next on the way.'

On the way back, Alexander pulled off the main road. Katherine looked at him, surprised. 'Where are we going?'

'Neither of us have eaten since the rolls we had for lunch. I don't know about you but my brain doesn't work unless it's kept fuelled.'

Katherine had to agree. Now that he'd mentioned food she realised she was ravenous.

A short while later he stopped at a small taverna with tables set out on a veranda upstairs. Despite the hour, and its location, it was thronged with people enjoying meals and drinks in the cool evening breeze of the mountains. Alexander led her over to a table away from the other diners. The view was spectacular. In the crevasses of the mountain hundreds of lights glittered a snaking path downwards towards the sea. When the waitress came Alexander raised his eyebrow in Katherine's direction.

'You order,' she said, reading his meaning. 'I don't care what I eat as long as it's filling.'

Alexander rattled off something in Greek so

rapidly she couldn't follow. While he did so she studied him from under her lashes. His earlier tiredness seemed to have disappeared and his usual energy was back. Although she was exhausted, she felt it too. Perhaps it was the urgency of the situation, the need to find answers that was making them both restless.

'So, what next?' Alexander asked, after the waiter had placed their meals in front of them. He'd ordered moussaka and a Greek salad to share. She speared a chunk of tomato on her fork and popped it into her mouth. Delicious.

'We should check in with Public Health in Athens and see if any more cases have been reported.' She laid her fork down, rummaged in her bag, pulled out her mini-laptop and fired it up. 'While you were in with David's parents I made some notes.' She moved it so he could see the screen.

'I've made a table. In the first column I've put the patient's name, the second has the date when they first came to the attention of the medical services and the third has a list of immediate family and friends and anyone else we know of who might have come into contact with them. It's not complete yet—there's bound to be names missing. Next to each name on the list is a column indicating whether they have been given prophylactic antibiotics. The last column is for places they have been in the last couple of weeks and will include swimming clubs, parties, et cetera. By creating a database I can sort the information any way I want. Sooner or later I'm hoping a common link will leap out. In the meantime, I've emailed a copy to my opposite number in Athens.'

Alexander looked impressed. 'You did all that? In, what? A couple of hours. Less.'

Warmth spread through her. Her reaction to him confused her. She couldn't remember a time when she'd felt more at ease in someone's company, yet at the same time her heart raced all the time she was with him.

'It's what I've been trained to do. If I were back at the hospital I'd have access to much more sophisticated programs to do it. On the other hand, entering the data myself helps me to understand it.'

He frowned. 'Is that what they've become? Data?'

'Of course they're not simply data,' Katherine retorted, stung. 'I'm a doctor but also a scientist. Trust me, this is the best way to approach this. Getting too close to individual patients can hinder a person when it comes to seeing patterns.' Hurt, she lowered her glass and pushed her half-eaten meal away. Her appetite had deserted her. 'Give me a moment, will you?' And without waiting for a reply, she stalked away.

Hearing footsteps behind her, Katherine turned. Somehow she wasn't surprised to find Alexander standing behind her.

'Aren't you cold?' he said softly.

'No. It's a perfect evening,' she murmured.

'May I join you?' he asked. When she nodded, he sat down next to her. She could smell his aftershave, almost feel the heat radiating from his body.

'I'm sorry,' he said. 'That was a stupid thing to say. I know you don't see the patients as data,' He grinned sheepishly. 'I'm perfectly aware that underneath the scientist façade beats a soft heart.' He placed a hand over hers. 'Will you forgive me?'

Her heart started pounding so hard she could barely breathe. What was it about him that made her feel that a whole world of possibility lay out there somewhere? She'd accepted that she would remain alone for the rest of her life, which, apart from the sorrow of her parents' deaths and a deep regret about the life she might have had had she made different choices, was a happy one. Then why did she feel she'd been fooling herself all this time?

'What are those lights out at sea?' she asked, to break the tension.

'It's the fishermen. A lot of them like to fish at night.'

'What about you? Is that what you use your boat for? I don't think I've ever seen you go out in it.'

He smiled. 'I've been waiting until I finished repainting it. But normally I go out in it whenever I can. Not just for fishing. I use it to island-hop sometimes. I like taking care of it. It belonged to my father once.' After a pause he continued, his voice soft and reflective. 'When I was a kid and we came to Greece on holiday I used to go out fishing at night with my uncle. Once he wouldn't take me—I forget the reason why. Perhaps he had other plans—but I wanted to go. There was a full moon and only a slight wind—perfect fishing weather. So I waited until everyone was asleep, then I crept out and launched my boat.'

She smiled, imagining the scene. 'Did you catch anything?'

'Tons. There were so many fish I forgot to think about where the boat was, and didn't notice it was drifting. When I looked up I couldn't see the lights on the shore any more.'

'What did you do?'

'I don't know what I was more scared of,' he said, 'being dragged out to the middle of the sea or my father's wrath when he found out I'd been out on my own. I knew the stars pretty well.' He pointed to the sky. 'I knew if I followed the right star it would guide me back to shore. Maybe not here exactly but to somewhere where I could walk or hitch a lift home.'

'And did you?'

'There was only one problem. When I realised I had lost sight of the shore, I jumped to my feet and lost an oar overboard.'

'That must have been a bit of a pain.'

He laughed. 'It was. I tried using the one oar, paddling from one side then the other, but I soon realised that, given the zig-zagging course I was making, it would take days, not hours, to reach the shore. I nearly gave up then. I could have stayed where I was. They would have sent out boats to find me once they discovered I was missing.'

'It's a big sea.'

'And even bigger when you're out there on your own.'

'Were you scared?'

'The thing was, except for the first scary moment, I wasn't. I knew my father would move heaven and earth to find me. I knew whether it took him the rest of his life, whether he had to spend every drachma he had to employ helicopters and search boats to find me, he would.'

'He must have loved you very much.'

'More than life itself.' He turned his head to look at her. 'A parent's love is the strongest love of all. It's only when you have a child yourself that you realise that.'

His words were like a knife straight to her heart. She clasped her hands together and squeezed. He couldn't know how much they hurt her.

'Is that what happened? Did he call the emergency services out?' She was relieved to find her voice sounded normal—cool even.

'No. Thank God he didn't have to. Despite my years in England, I was a Greek boy brought up on legends and myths about Greek heroes. There was no chance I was going to wait for him to come searching for me. I would have died rather than sit there waiting meekly for rescue.' Although he sounded indignant, she could hear the laughter in his voice.

'So, what *did* you do?'

'I decided to try and swim back.'

She laughed. 'You're kidding!'

'It was madness. I know that now, but back then it was all I could think of doing. However I couldn't leave the boat to float out to sea. It was my father's pride and joy. So I threw the fish back. It almost killed me. A whole night's work and the best catch I'd ever had! I jumped out of the boat and, keeping hold of the rope, I swam back to shore.'

'You could have drowned.'

'I knew as long as I kept hold of the boat, I'd be all right. And it worked. It took me a bloody long time but I made it into a small bay just as the sun was coming up. But I still had to get the damned boat back to its proper mooring. So I nicked one of the oars from a boat that was in the bay and rowed home. I've never rowed as fast in all my life. I was determined to get home before my father noticed I was gone.'

'And did you?'

He smiled ruefully. 'Now, that was the thing. I did. At least I thought I did. I crept into bed and a few moments later I heard my father get up. I was pretty pleased with myself, I can tell you. But later, when I went down to the boat again just to check there wasn't any evidence of my night-time excursion, the oar I had pinched was missing and there, in its place, was a brand-new one.' He sighed.

'He must have known what I was up to all along. I bet he was sitting on the wall all night, waiting for me to come home. When he knew I was safe he must have hurried back to bed, and then, when he was sure I was asleep, gone down to check on the boat. Of course, he would have seen instantly that one of the oars had come from another boat and so he made a new one. And you know...' he paused and looked out to sea '...he never once mentioned it. Not ever.'

They sat in silence for a while. 'It sounds as if you have always been surrounded by your family's love. No wonder Crystal is such a happy little girl.'

He looked into the distance. 'I've been lucky, I guess, in so many ways. But the gods like to even the score.' He could only be talking about his wife.

'What about you?' he continued. 'Did you have a happy childhood too?'

Perhaps it was his Greek upbringing that made him talk like this? Most British men she knew would rather die a hundred deaths then talk about their feelings. Or perhaps it was the night—perhaps everyone found it easier to talk under the cover of darkness.

'Of course my parents loved me. It's just that I think I disappointed them.' The words were out before she knew it.

'Disappointed them? The dedicated, bursary-winning scholar? Did you go off the rails or something when you were a teenager?' He shook his head. 'No, I can't see it. I bet you were head girl.'

Going off the rails was one way of putting it. Off track for a while was perhaps closer to the truth.

She shook her head. 'I was never that popular. Far too studious and serious. I was a prefect, though.'

'There. I was right. And then you went to medical school and here you are about to submit your thesis for your doctorate and one of Europe's top specialists in the spread of infectious diseases. What is there not to be proud of?'

Judging by the teasing note in his voice, he couldn't have known how close to the bone he had come with his questions. She scrambled to her feet. 'I am getting a little cold. I think it's time we went on our way.'

Later that night, she lay in bed listening to the gentle rush of the waves on the shore and thinking about what Alexander had said. She'd tried so hard to make her parents proud, and to an extent she had. Her mother had told anyone who'd listen, sometimes complete strangers, that her daughter was a doctor. In fact, to hear her mother speak you'd think that her daughter was single-handedly responsible for the health of the nation. But what she had wanted most of all, a grandchild she could fuss over, Katherine hadn't given her.

Throwing the covers aside, she went out to the balcony. Alexander was making her think about stuff she didn't want to think about, like loss, and families—and love.

Love. What would it like to be loved by Alexander? It hit her then—she wasn't just attracted to him, she was falling in love with him.

Of all men, why did it have to be him? He was still in love with his wife, that much was obvious. And even if he wasn't, his life was here in Greece and she'd be returning to the UK to pick up hers. But worst of all, if he knew her secret he would despise her. He would never understand why she'd done what she had.

She returned to the sitting room and flicked through the playlist on her iPod. She inserted it into the speakers she had brought with her and as the sound of Brahms filled the room she sat on the sofa and closed her eyes.

* * *

What was it with him and this woman? Alexander thought as he stared at the stars from his bedroom window. Why couldn't he stop thinking about her? It wasn't as if he had any intention of having a relationship with her. No one would ever take Sophia's place. Katherine would be returning to the UK soon and he couldn't follow her, she was as much married to her work as he was—there were a hundred different reasons.

Yet he couldn't fool himself any longer that he wasn't strongly attracted to her. Perhaps because he saw his own sadness reflected in her eyes? Or was it because, despite her protestations, he suspected she was lonely and he knew only too well how that felt? It was only when she talked about her work that her reserve disappeared. Her eyes shone and she became more animated. He liked it that she felt passionately about what she did—in many ways she reminded him of the way he used to be. And look how that had turned out.

His mind shied away from the past and back to Katherine.

He liked everything about her—the way she looked, her sensitivity and reserve, the sudden smile that lit up her face, banishing the shadows in her eyes, the way she was with Crystal, slightly awkward but not talking down to her the way many adults did, how she was with Yia-Yia and the villagers: respectful, but not patronising.

When the realisation hit him it was like jumping into a pool of water from a height. Shock then exhilaration. He didn't just like her—he was falling in love with her.

As the plaintive notes of Brahms's Lullaby filtered through the still night air from the other side of the square he went outside and listened. It had been one of Sophia's favourites—something she'd played often. He closed his eyes as an image of Sophia rushed back, her head bent over the keys of the piano, her hair falling forward as her fingers flew over the keys, a smile of pure happiness on her lips. His chest tightened. Sophia. His love. How could he think, even for a moment, that there could ever be anyone else?

CHAPTER SIX

COMFORTED BY THE soothing strains of the music and knowing sleep would elude her, Katherine studied her database, entering the list of names Alexander had given her.

She stopped when she came to Stéfan's name. He had been the first patient to fall ill. Concentrating on him was key.

There was something about him that was tugging at her memory. What was it? Yes! She had it. The day he'd collapsed at the surgery, he'd been sporting a bandage on his right hand. And it hadn't been clean either. It had looked professional, though. Someone had bandaged his hand but not recently. Hercules leaped onto her lap and started purring. She stroked him absentmindedly as she dialled Alexander's phone. Despite the late hour, he picked up immediately.

'The boy who died. Stéfan Popalopadous? Do you know how he hurt his hand? Did he have it dressed at your practice?' she asked, coming straight to the point.

Alexander mumbled a curse under his breath. 'Hello to you too. No, I don't know how Stéfan hurt his hand. Not without looking at his notes, which, of course, are at the practice. But something tells me that's where I'm going.'

'Would you like me to come with you?' she asked.

'No. That's okay. Keep your phone near you and I'll call you as soon as I have an answer.'

It was over an hour before he called back. She snatched up the phone. 'Yes? What have you found out?'

'He damaged his hand in a winch on his boat. Apparently he often takes people out for trips in the evenings after work. He was treated in Nafplio. He runs trips between there and all the major ports along the coast.'

'Then Nafplio is where we're going. Pick me up on the way.'

Nafplio was pretty, with elegant town houses with balconies that reminded her of Venice. Alexander told her a little of the town's history on the way. During the Ottoman era it had once been the capital of Greece and the Palamayde fortress, which dominated the town, had been a prison during the Greek War of Independence. Now the town was a stopover for some of the smaller cruise ships on their way around the Mediterranean as well as for yachts either in flotillas or in singles. That wasn't good: If one of the transient visitors had come into contact with their patient, who knew where they would be now? Was that how Claire had contracted the disease?

They phoned the doctor of the surgery where Stéfan's hand had been dressed, rousing him from his bed, and discovered that they'd been right. Stéfan had been treated there a couple of days before he'd turned up at Alexander's practice. He'd had a temperature, but it hadn't been raised enough to cause concern.

Now they had their first contact, they could be reasonably confident of tracing the others before they became sick.

Katherine and Alexander exchanged high-fives as soon as they left the practice. 'You're some public health doctor,' he said.

She grinned back at him. 'I am, aren't I?'

Over the next week, Katherine and Alexander visited all the villages and towns where cases of meningitis had been reported, as well as those of all the contacts they'd traced. Now they knew about Stéfan, it was easier to trace the people he'd come into contact with and their contacts. David, the boy in Intensive Care, had been taken around the coast with a number of his friends as a birthday treat, and the other eight victims, most of whom were recovering, had also taken trips in Stéfan's boat in the days before Stéfan had become unwell. Finally Claire's parents confirmed that their daughter had posted a photo on her Facebook page of Stéfan and his boat shortly before she'd become ill.

Katherine and Alexander set up temporary clinics and spoke to the local nurses and medical staff, advising them what to look out for and what information to give their patients. There had been one new case, but as everyone was more vigilant, she had been admitted to hospital as soon as she'd started showing symptoms and was doing well.

The longer she worked with Alexander the more she admired him. He was good with the patients, kind and understanding with panicked villagers, and authoritative with those who needed to be persuaded to take the antibiotics. It was tiring work and they spent hours in the car, driving from village to village, but she treasured those times most of all. They spoke of their day, what they had to do next, but they also talked about the music they liked and places they wanted to visit.

However, she was aware he was holding back from her, as she was from him. Often it was on the tip of her tongue to tell him about Poppy but the time never seemed right, or, if she was honest, she was too frightened of his reaction. What would he think if, or when, she did tell him? Would he be shocked? Or would he understand? And why tell him anyway? As long as there were no new cases of meningitis she would be leaving at the end of September and so far he'd said nothing, done nothing to make her think he saw her as more than a friend and colleague—albeit one he was attracted to.

She'd caught him looking at her when she'd been sneaking looks in his direction. Unsure of what it meant, she'd dropped her eyes, her pulse racing, finding an excuse to turn away, to speak to someone else.

But apart from the looks, he'd never as much as taken her hand or kissed her good-night. She suspected he was still in love with his dead wife and that no woman would ever live up to her.

The thought of returning to the UK made her heart ache. To leave all this when she'd only just found it. To go back to a life that more than ever seemed colourless and grey. To leave Alexander, his grandmother and Crystal—most of all Alexander—was breaking her heart.

Perhaps it was being here in Greece? Perhaps it was just the magic spell the country had woven around her? Maybe when she returned to the UK she'd be able to see it for what it was: infatuation, brought on by too much sun and the joy of working with someone who cared about what he did as much as she.

But she knew she was fooling herself. She wasn't just falling in love with him—she loved him—totally, deeply and would love him for as long as she breathed. But, he didn't love her. Nothing and no one could replace his wife. His life was here with his daughter and his family while hers was back in London.

And what if he suspected how she felt about him? That would be too humiliating. Maybe he'd already guessed?.

She threw down her book and started pacing. Perhaps he thought she visited his house as a means to get close to him. And going to the square every evening to share a meal or a beer with him. Wasn't that practically admitting she couldn't stay away from him? God, she'd done everything but drool whenever he was near. She'd virtually thrown herself at him. How could she have been so stupid?

Well, there was only one way to rectify that. She would keep her distance. She wouldn't visit Yia-Yia, she wouldn't go to the square. If anyone asked she would say she was behind with her thesis. That, as it happened, was perfectly true. Besides, what did she care if anyone—least of all him—thought she was making excuses? As long as they didn't think she was some desperate woman trying to snag the local widowed doctor while she was here.

But not to see him? Except in passing? To even think it tore her in two.

She should have known this kind of happiness couldn't last.

Alexander stood on the balcony, a glass of cold water in his hand, his thoughts straying, as they always did these days, to Katherine. He hadn't seen much of her since they'd stopped visiting the affected villages and he missed her. She used to come most evenings to the square but she hadn't been for a while. Was she avoiding him?

Working with her these last weeks he'd come to admire her more and more. She was good at what she did. Very good. If she hadn't been around he doubted that they would have got on top of the outbreak as quickly as they had. Her patience with the affected families, her manner towards the villagers, her determination to speak her faltering Greek to them and the kindness and respect with which she treated young and old alike was very much the Greek ethos. He loved how her forehead furrowed when she was thinking, how her face lit up when she laughed, and most of all the way she was with Crystal. His daughter adored her.

Katherine was almost as perfect in her way as Sophia had been in hers. But she'd be going soon. And the thought of not seeing her again filled him with dismay.

It hit him then. He didn't just like and admire Katherine, he was crazy about her.

So what was he doing here, on his own, kicking his heels when he could be with her?

CHAPTER SEVEN

KATHERINE WAS SITTING on her balcony, watching the sun cast shadows on the sea, when she heard a soft tap on the door. Having come to recognise the sound of Alexander's footsteps, she didn't need to turn around to know it was him. Neither was she really surprised. Deep down she'd known it was only a matter of time before he sought her out.

'Crystal's been looking for you at the taverna these last couple of evenings,' he said softly. 'So was I. And Yia-Yia says she hasn't seen you for a day or two. Are you all right? Not ill or anything?'

The way he was searching her face made her pulse skip a beat.

'I thought I should give company a miss for a while.' Her heart was thumping so hard she was finding it difficult to breathe. 'With everything that has happened, I've fallen behind with my thesis. I'm planning to submit it in the next couple of days.'

He came to sit in the chair next to hers. 'When do you leave?'

'At the end of the month. There's nothing to keep me here longer now the epidemic seems to be under control. I had a phone call from Athens earlier—there's been no more cases reported in the last forty-eight hours. They're pretty confident the outbreak is over.'

'Thank God. If you hadn't got onto it as soon as you did, there could have been more deaths.'

'I was only doing my job. A job I love.'

His expression was unreadable in the light of the moon.

'I never did take you out on the boat, did I?' he said softly.

'No, you didn't,' she agreed. 'But you've been busy. It can't be easy for you, working and being a single father.' God, couldn't she think of anything less inane to say?

'I have Yia-Yia. And Helen when I need her.' He hooked his hands behind his head. 'Although as Helen's getting married in a few weeks it's unlikely that Crystal and I will see as much of her.' He leaned forward. 'I could still take you out on the boat. In fact, we could go later tonight. It's a perfect night for it.'

She didn't think it was possible for her heart to beat any faster but apparently it could.

'You don't have to take me, you know,' she said stiffly.

He looked taken aback. 'Of course I don't have to take you. Why would you think that?' His eyes locked on hers. 'It's not just Crystal who's missed you, I've missed spending time with you too,' he said softly. 'I like being with you. Haven't you realised that by now?' He stood and reached out a hand for hers.

Her heart beating a tattoo against her ribs, she allowed him to pull her to her feet. For a moment she swayed towards him, driven by a need to feel his arms around her. At the last moment she stopped herself and took a step back. Hadn't she told herself she wouldn't make a fool of herself?

He looked bemused, as well he might. How could he know what was inside her head when she barely did? However, he didn't let go of her hand.

'We should wait until Crystal's asleep, though,' he continued, 'otherwise she'll insist on coming too. If I say no, I wouldn't put it past her to launch a boat of her own and come after us.'

Katherine had to laugh, even if it sounded shaky. 'No one can say she's not your daughter.'

'No.' His expression grew more serious. 'I could do with having you on my own for a bit. My daughter has taken such a liking to you, it's difficult to prise her from your side.'

Her heart catapulted inside her chest.

Why was she worrying about the future? It felt right that he was here, and why not sleep with him if he asked? And she was certain he would ask. She would be leaving soon and although there was no chance of a future for them, why resist snatching a few days of happiness? He need never know her secret. What mattered was here and now and if she could be with him, even for a short while, why not? She'd have plenty time to lick her wounds—to regret what could have been—when she left here. She surprised herself. Greece had changed so much about her.

'We should make the most of what time you have left,' he said, as if reading her mind. 'I could take some leave. We could spend it together.'

'And Crystal? Isn't she expecting to spend time with you?'

'Of course. And she will. I thought the three of us could do some stuff.' He searched her face. 'I know having my daughter around, adorable though she is, puts a spanner in the works, but happily she does go to sleep in the evenings. You do like her, don't you? She's definitely taken a shine to you.'

She wanted to ask him whether he liked to be with her because of Crystal because, much as she was coming to love the little girl, she needed him to want to be with her. But she wouldn't ask him. And what if he said yes? What if he asked her to stay permanently? What would she do then? At the very least she would have to admit that there was a very large part of her life she was keeping secret from him. Perhaps the time to tell him was now, before they got in any deeper. But if she did, what would he say? How would he react?

And what was she thinking anyway? Even if he did ask her to stay, she wouldn't. She couldn't. How could she take on the care of a child after what she'd done? However, didn't he deserve the truth from her, whether she stayed or not?

She was being given a glimpse of a life she might have. A chance to break free from the strait-jacket of the one she'd imposed on herself with its rules, self-denial, hard work and determination. Could she forgive herself—allow herself the joy of loving and being loved? Even for a short while.

He misinterpreted her silence and stood. 'I'll see you about then?'

'What time do you want me to meet you?'

His expression lightened. 'About ten?'

'I'll be there.'

When she arrived at the bay he was leaning against the boat, wearing a black T-shirt and dark jeans with fisherman's boots. He looks a bit like a pirate, she thought, especially with the five o'clock shadow darkening his jaw. He whistled appreciatively when he saw her. She'd been like a cat on a hot tin roof all evening. After discarding several outfits, she'd finally settled on a pair of faded denim shorts and a cheesecloth embroidered blouse she'd purchased in the village. Underneath she wore a lacy bra with matching panties. She'd shaved her legs and moisturised all over.

She couldn't remember the last time she'd felt so nervous and was ready long before she was due to meet him. Unable to change the habits of a lifetime, she'd packed a small bag with a cardigan in the unlikely event it was chilly on the water, and at the last minute had added some fresh fruit and olives, a bottle of wine, a corkscrew and two glasses. It was always better to be prepared.

'Hello,' she whispered. Feeling inexplicably like a naughty child, she suppressed the desire to giggle.

'You don't have to whisper, you know,' he said with a grin. 'It's not as if we're ten years old and stealing a boat.'

'Sorry,' she said in a normal voice. 'Whispering just seemed to go with the moment.'

The boat was in the water, where it drifted gently in the waves, and he was holding on to the rope to stop it being pushed out to sea. 'Why don't you climb in?' he suggested.

She slipped off her sandals and stepped into the sea, shivering as the waves lapped around her ankles, then her calves and above her knees. As her skin adjusted to the temperature, the cool water felt delicious against her overheated skin.

But once she'd reached the boat she stood dumbfounded. How was she supposed to get in? As if reading her mind, Alexander, still holding the rope but gathering it in towards him, waded over until he was standing next to her. Suddenly she felt a pair of strong hands circle her waist and then she was off her feet and he was holding her in his arms. Even in the warmth of the evening air she was conscious of the heat radiating from his body and the clean, fresh scent of him.

He laughed down at her. 'Good thing you weigh

nothing.' A slight exaggeration, she thought—she wasn't the smallest of women—but then she was being dropped gently into the boat. A few seconds later Alexander sprang in alongside her. Tentatively she took a seat at the back. He picked up an oar and pushed them away from the shore, before coiling the rope into a neat round and placing it on the bottom of the boat. 'Sit in the front if you like,' he said. 'No, not now!' he added as she stood, making the boat wobble. 'Wait until we're a bit further out. Unless you want us to both end up in the water?'

Feeling a little foolish, she sat back down as Alexander started rowing. The moon was so bright she could see the muscles of his arms bunching with every pull of the oar.

'Are we going to fish?' she asked.

'If you like. But later. I want to show you something first.'

A comfortable silence fell, punctuated only by the creak of the boat against the oars and the lapping of the sea. Katherine trailed her hand in the water.

'Watch out for sharks,' he cautioned.

She pulled her hand out of the water as if she'd had an electric shock. But when she looked at him she saw, from his grin, that he'd been teasing her.

Her skin tingled and she grinned back at him. How she loved this man!

'So, what is it you want to show me?'

'I'm afraid you're going to have to wait and see.' He refused to say any more so she let herself relax, gasping with delight as a shooting star sped across the sky before falling towards the black depths of the ocean. It was if she had been transported into a different world. Happiness surged through her. Everything about being here—being with Alexander—made her feel more alive than she'd ever felt before. As if the person she was when she was with him was a different, more together version of herself on one hand and a wilder, more interesting, version on the other.

It must have been so hard for her mother to leave here when she married. Britain was a colder, greyer place than the one she'd left. Although the way the villagers lived, almost on top of each other and constantly visiting each other's homes, had taken Katherine time to get used to, and she could see how someone used to living in such close proximity with their neighbours, always having someone to call on for support, would struggle to adapt in a strange country with an entirely different culture. Her mother had loved her father very much and, as she'd told Katherine often, she would rather have been with Dad in hell than without him.

A wave of sadness threatened to swamp her mood. At least she was here. In the country her mother had once called home, she felt nearer to her than she'd felt since she'd died.

'You okay?'

Alexander's voice jerked her back to the present. 'Yes. Why?'

'It's just that you looked sad there for a moment.'

She forced a smile. 'Just thinking about my mother and wishing she'd been able come back even once before she died.'

In the distance the tiny lights from other boats bobbed on the sea. Beyond them dark shapes of small islands broke up the horizon.

'Perhaps *you'll* come back—or stay?' he said softly.

Her pulse upped another notch. Was he asking her to?

'I have my work. But, yes, I think will. What about you? Do you think you might ever return to the UK?' She held her breath as she waited for his answer.

'To visit my mother certainly. But I couldn't leave Greece permanently. I couldn't take Crystal away from her grandmother. At least, not until she's older.'

Her earlier happiness dimmed. She could understand him not wanting to separate Crystal from her great-grandmother, not until she was older anyway, but if he felt about Katherine the way she felt about him, wouldn't he want to be with her? Wouldn't he ask her outright to stay?

'Why,' he continued, 'do we always regret what might have been instead of being grateful for the life we have?'

Her heart thudded a tattoo against her chest. She wanted to ask him what he meant. Was he referring to her? What might have been? Or was he talking about his wife?

'Do you regret coming back here?' she asked instead.

'Not at all. It was the right decision for Crystal. Anyway, the UK was too—' He stopped suddenly. 'Too cold,' he finished. She was sure that wasn't what he had been about to say. In unguarded moments his sadness mirrored her own. Even after two years he was still grieving for his wife. But he should find some comfort in the knowledge he had found love—a great love, she suspected—and she envied him for it. More, she envied the woman who had been the recipient.

They lapsed into silence again. Just when she was beginning to wonder where exactly he was taking her, an island with a small bay came into view.

'Is this the place you wanted to show me?' she asked.

'Greece has many beautiful islands, but this is one I like to come to whenever I take out the boat. Not least because no one ever comes here. The only other place I like more is Cape Sounion.'

'Where's that?'

'You mean you don't know? You must have heard of the temple of Poseidon. It's where Byron used to go to write his poetry. I'll take you one day.'

His assumption that they would be spending more time together sent a ripple of happiness through her. She'd waited how many years to find someone like him and she'd had to come to a remote part of Greece to do so. If only she had an inkling of how he felt about her. If only he could love her the way he had loved, and probably still loved, his wife; if only she could make him understand why she'd done what she had, they might have a chance of a future together.

But he would never understand. She was certain of that.

He jumped out of the boat, holding its rope, and held out his arms. She let him swing her into them. As his arms tightened around her she closed her eyes, wanting to savour every last moment. He carried her ashore before standing her gently on her feet.

'So, what's so special about this island?' she asked, when he returned from pulling the boat out of the water. 'You've just told me Greece has hundreds of beautiful islands.'

'Legend has it that a Spartan soldier brought a Trojan princess here when he captured her. I have no evidence that this is the exact place,' he said, holding his hands up as if to ward off her protests, 'but he described it as an island not far from my village whose beauty was only dimmed by the beauty of his wife.' His voice dropped to a murmur. 'He believed if he kept her here, safe, nothing bad would ever happen to her and they could live out the rest of their lives together and in peace.'

'And did they? In your story?' It might only be a legend but she really wanted to know.

His gaze returned to hers, the tone of his voice almost dismissive. 'No. In time he got bored. He missed the excitement and prestige that came with being in the Greek army.'

'What happened?'

'When he was away, fighting in some war or another, his enemies found her here. They captured her and intended to make her a consort. She guessed what they planned so when they weren't watching her, she escaped and ran to the cliff. She threw herself into the sea.'

'Oh, no! And what happened to her lover?'

'As soon as he came back and discovered what had happened, he went mad with grief and guilt. He drowned himself so he could be with her in death.'

Katherine shivered. 'That's so sad.'

He reached for her hand. 'What do you think he should have done? Was he not wrong to bring her here where she was alone and unprotected?' His eyes bored into hers as if her answer really mattered. 'Don't you think he deserved what happened?'

'Well, first of all,' she began cautiously, her reaction was her choice. I don't think she would have agreed to come and live here with him if she hadn't wanted to. She must have known he was trying to protect her the best way he knew how. In the end he was wrong, but that doesn't mean he didn't do what he did for the right reasons. Didn't you say earlier that there is no point regretting what might have been?'

She knew she was talking as much about her own situation as this mythical couple's. 'It's easy to look back on our lives and see what we did wrong, what we should have done—but at the time we can only make the best decision we can in the circumstances.'

'Is that what you really believe? I can't imagine you have much to regret.'

This conversation was getting too close to the bone for comfort. Perhaps it was time to tell him about Poppy. But fear held her back. She couldn't bear it if he judged her or, worse, rejected her. She forced a smile. 'Why do you like the island so much if it has such a sad story attached to it?'

He poured her some wine and passed the glass to her. The touch of his fingertips brushing against hers sent hot sparks up her arm. 'In a way, I guess it is sad. But legend has it that the gods took pity on them and turned them into dolphins. I like to think of them out in the ocean together—always.'

Her heart twisted. So she'd been right. He was still in love with his wife.

He stepped forward and took her face between his hands. 'I don't know why no man has captured you yet. What is wrong with English men?'

'Perhaps it is me,' she said, then could have kicked herself. It was difficult to think straight with him being so close. 'I mean, being too picky.'

He laughed down at her, his teeth white in the dark. 'You should be picky,' he said. He tangled his hands in her hair and, with his thumbs under her cheek bones, raised her face to his. 'You are so beautiful. So perfect.'

No, she thought wildly. *Don't think that!* He mustn't think she was perfect. He'd only be disappointed.

He lowered his head and brought his mouth down on hers and then she couldn't think any more. This was what she'd been imagining almost from the moment she'd first set eyes on him and it was everything she'd dreamed it would be. As his kisses deepened she clung to him, almost dizzy with desire.

When he moved away she gave a little gasp of disappointment. But he lifted her in his arms and carried her over to a soft patch of grass where he laid her down.

'Are you sure?' he asked as she gazed up at him.

'Sure?' She almost laughed. She pulled him down to her. 'What took you so long?' she murmured against his lips.

* * *

Later, they lay wrapped in each other's arms, gazing up at the stars. She'd never felt so peaceful, so thoroughly made love to. He'd been demanding, gentle and teasing and had touched her in ways she couldn't remember being touched before, until she'd cried out with her need to have him inside her. She blushed as she remembered how she'd dug her fingertips into his back, how she'd called out to him as wave upon wave of pleasure had rocked her body.

But she didn't really care. This wanton, this woman he'd unleashed, was a revelation to her and she never wanted to go back to the one she'd been before. She smiled to herself. This was what sex should be like.

The moonlight shone on his naked body. It was every bit as she'd imagined—better than any of the Greek statues she'd seen. No wonder she hadn't been able to stop thinking about how he would feel under her hands. A smile curved her lips and she laughed with sheer joy.

He propped himself on his elbow and gazed down at her. Instinctively she reached for her blouse to cover her nakedness, but as she moved her hand he caught it in his fingers. 'Don't,' he murmured. 'I don't think I could ever get enough of just looking at you.'

The new wanton Katherine revelled in the desire she saw in his eyes.

She reached up to him and wrapped her arms around his neck.

As the horizon turned pink and apricot they lay in each other's arms, looking up at the star-sprinkled sky, their hands entwined. 'There's something I need to tell you,' he said softly.

Oh, God, here it was. *This was wonderful but...*

'Remember I told you that I was training to be a surgeon when Sophia died,' he continued.

'Yes.'

'And I said I was working all the time?'

She wasn't sure where this was going. 'I know how competitive the speciality can be.'

'When Sophia fell pregnant with Crystal I was so happy. And so was she. If at times I caught her looking wistful I just put it down to her being homesick for Greece. It suited me to believe that's all it was. Looking back, I think she knew it was the end of her dream to become a concert pianist.

'I was determined to make it in surgery, but you know how it is—the competition is fierce, especially for the top positions, and only the best job in the most prestigious hospital would do me. I had it all planned out. I would qualify for a consultant post then I would apply to the Mayo Clinic in America and do some further training there. I'd already sat my board exams when I was a resident in my final year at med school so getting a post wouldn't be an issue as long as I stayed focussed.

'Sophia backed me all the way. She said she could play her music anywhere. I knew that wasn't necessarily true—not if she wanted to play professionally—but I chose not to listen to that particular voice. I was a selfish bastard back then—completely focussed on what I wanted to achieve. I told myself I was doing it for all of us, for me, for Sophia—and for the baby on the way.

'What I chose to forget was that she'd already put her career on hold for me. A musician's career is, if anything, more competitive than medicine—they have such a short time to "make it" and she'd already jeopardised her chances by coming with me to the UK. But, as I said, I planned to make it up to her. One day when I'd got to where I needed to go, I would slow down, let my career take a back seat and let her enjoy the limelight for a while.

'We both wanted a family and I told myself that by the time I had reached the top, the children would be of an age to allow her time for herself. There was always going to be more than one child. We both wanted at least three. Call me clever, huh? If I'd done the math I would have realised that if everything went to plan she would have been thirty three by the time the youngest was born. I thought it was simple. We'd have children. Sophia would stay at home until the youngest was six weeks or so and then we'd employ a nanny. And Sophia went along with it. Until Crystal was born. Then she could no more see herself putting any child of hers into a nursery than she could have left them home alone. She loved being a mother. If she found it boring she never said so and I never asked.

'She always made friends easily and the house was always filled—at least so I heard as I was rarely home long enough to see for myself. It was as if she'd gathered around her friends to be the family she'd left behind in Greece. I told myself she was happy. But when I thought about it later, I couldn't remember the last time she'd played the piano. At the time I told myself that that was good—that she wasn't really driven enough to make it as a concert pianist. Why is everything so much more obvious in hindsight?'

Katherine rolled over so she could see his

face. 'We all see things differently later, don't we?' she murmured, although every word he'd said about Sophia cut her like a blade.

'I never stopped loving her. She was my best friend, my lover, the mother of my child, but I stopped seeing her—really seeing her.'

The sadness in his eyes twisted her heart.

'She deserved more than I gave her. Perhaps I didn't love her enough. If I had I wouldn't have put my needs so far above hers.'

'She was lucky to be loved the way you loved her. She would have known she was deeply loved,' Katherine whispered.

'I'm glad you told me about her.' And she was. She wanted to know everything about him. Even if hearing about how much he'd loved Sophia hurt.

'I had to. You have to know why I'm not sure I can ever promise more than what we have here tonight. I care too much about you not to tell you the truth about myself. And there's more...'

She stopped his words with her fingertips. The here and now was all they had. After what he'd told her, how could she ever tell him about Poppy? And not telling him meant they could never have more than what they had now. 'Let's not think about the past,' she said. 'Let's only think about now.' She moved her hand from his lips and taking his head between her palms lowered herself on top of him.

When they returned to the village she led him by the hand up the path and into her home. Her heart was beating so fast she couldn't speak.

He kicked the door closed behind him. '*Agapi-mou*,' he breathed into her neck. 'I want you. I need you.'

She stepped into his arms feeling as if, at last, she'd come home—even if only for a while.

They spent every day of the next week with each other, until Alexander's leave was over. Crystal came to the house often. If Katherine was working, the child would take the colouring book she'd brought with her and lay it on the table next to Katherine's papers, and quietly, her tongue caught in the corner of her mouth, use her crayons to colour in, stopping periodically to admire her work or to study Katherine from the corner of her eye, waiting patiently until Katherine stopped what she was doing to admire her efforts. Increasingly, Katherine would find herself, at Yia-Yia's invitation, at the family home, pitching in to make olive tapenade or some other Greek dish. Then, instead of sitting and looking out at the beach, they'd retire to the bench at the front of the house and sit in silence, enjoying the heat of the sun and letting the ebb and flow of village life happen around them. Katherine's rusty Greek was improving by leaps and bounds and she and Alexander's grandmother were able to communicate reasonably well.

She'd also become confident enough with her Greek to stop to chat with the other villagers when she was passing through the square. Soon small gifts of ripe tomatoes and zucchini, enormous squashes and bunches of fat grapes still on the vine appeared on her doorstep, and before long she had more plump olives than she could hope ever to eat and more bottles of home-made olive oil than she knew what to do with.

She often thought of her mother. It was as if she'd planned this, knowing that Greece would weave its magic around her and that Katherine would discover what she had missed out on in life. It was, Katherine realised, her mother's final gift to her and one she wanted to savour. As it had done during the epidemic, her thesis lay largely ignored—dotting the 'i's and crossing the 't's didn't seem as important as they once had—although Katherine knew she would never submit it until it was as perfect as she could make it. Greece hadn't turned her into a complete sloth.

But she *was* less than perfect here. She no longer blow-dried her hair every morning before twirling it into a tight bun. Instead she wore it lose around her shoulders or twisted carelessly into a ponytail, no longer caring if it frizzed a little around the edges. She felt freer without the tights, the buttoned-to-the-neck shirts, tailored trousers and sensible shoes she'd worn when she'd first arrived. Now it was bare-shouldered sundresses, skimpy shorts and strappy T-shirts. She'd even repainted her nails in the same blood red as Crystal had—leaving Crystal's handiwork would have been a step too far! With Alexander back at work, she saw little of him during the day, but most evenings they drank cold beer and nibbled olives and fresh figs, spoke about work and history while Crystal played in the square. He made her laugh with his amusing stories of the villagers and his patients and although her skin still fizzed every time he looked at her, she was able to relax in his company in a way that she hadn't done with anyone, apart from Sally, in years.

It was, Katherine thought, the happiest time of her life. For once, nothing was asked of her, nothing demanded, no one expected anything of her. Sometimes Crystal came with them and sometimes they went on their own. He took her to Cape Souinon and she could see straight away why he loved it. The ruins of the temple of Poseidon looked out towards the sea and she could easily imagine Lord Byron sitting with his back against one of the pillars, writing poetry.

Often they spent the day on the beach with Crystal, swimming, picnicking and sharing intimate smiles. In the evenings he would call at her house and together they would climb the path to the village square, releasing their hands by unspoken consent moments before they reached it. But it was the nights she longed for most. When his daughter was asleep he'd come to her house and they'd make love, either in her bed or down in the little bay. He'd wake up early and leave her to return to his home so that he'd always be there when Crystal woke up. And every day she fell just a little more in love with him.

She didn't know how she was ever going to say goodbye.

Alexander was whistling as he showered. In a short while he'd be seeing Katherine. It had been a long time, he reflected, since he'd felt this good. Not since Sophia had died.

And it was all down to Katherine. He grinned remembering the night before. How could he ever have thought she was reserved—when it came to making love she was anything but.

Unfortunately his lunchtime date with Katherine was going to be curtailed. He had a patient who needed a home visit. Perhaps Katherine would come with him? He didn't want to waste any of the little time they had left.

But why should she leave?

He stepped out of the shower.

She could come to live with him in Greece. He was certain she would find another job here easily. Or he could find one in England. He quickly dismissed the thought. He couldn't uproot Crystal again. At least not until she was older. Katherine would understand. She knew how important it was for Crystal to be brought up around family.

But would she stay? They would get married of course. The thought brought him up short. Marriage! He almost laughed out loud. He'd been so certain he'd never marry again, but that was before he'd met Katherine. Now he couldn't imagine the rest of his life without her.

Although she hadn't said, he was certain Katherine was in love with him. But enough to marry him? Give up her life in the UK?

There was only one way to find out. 'What do you think, Sophia?' he murmured. 'Do I deserve another chance at happiness?'

CHAPTER EIGHT

KATHERINE WAS PORING over her computer, trying and failing to concentrate on finishing her paper, when there was a knock on the door. No one in the village ever knocked and certainly not Crystal, and although she was expecting Alexander any minute, he always marched in, announcing himself by calling out her name. She quickly saved the file she was working on and went to answer.

When she saw who it was her heart almost stopped beating.

'Poppy?'

Her daughter pushed by her and dropped her rucksack on the floor. 'I'm surprised you know who I am.'

Admittedly, for a brief moment Katherine hadn't. Her daughter had changed so much since the last photo she had seen of her. Gone was her long, golden hair. Gone was the awkward yet beautiful, fresh-faced teenager. In her place was an angry-looking young woman with black spiky hair, kohl-ringed panda eyes and a lip-piercing.

'Of course I know who you are,' Katherine whispered. She'd dreamed of this moment for so long but in her imagination it had taken the form of getting-to-know-you phone calls followed by lunches and shopping trips. In her head, Poppy had been like her as a teenager; demure, well spoken and beautifully mannered. Nothing in her dreams had prepared her for this. But despite her dismay, a warm, happy glow was spreading from her stomach towards her heart.

Poppy flung herself down on the sofa. 'I thought you might be staying in a villa or something. But this place is pokey. I don't see a pool.'

'That's because there isn't one.' She was still stunned. 'But there's an ocean to swim in.'

'Oh, well. I suppose it will have to do. Anything's better than being at home with *them*.'

'Them?'

'Liz and Mike. The people who call themselves my parents.'

Katherine's head was whirling. 'How did you know I was here? Do Liz and Mike know you're with me?'

'I had your email address, remember? I emailed your work address and got an out-of-

office reply, so I phoned them and told them I needed to know where you were. I told them it was urgent—a family emergency—and luckily I got through to a receptionist who didn't know you had no family.' The last was said with heavy and pointed emphasis on the 'no'. 'And as for Mum and Dad, no. They don't know I'm here. They don't care where I am!'

'Poppy! They must be out of their minds with worry! You must—'

'All they care about is their new baby. It's Charlie this and Charlie that. God, why did they adopt me if they were going to go and have a baby of their own?'

Mike and Liz had had a baby? Well, it wasn't unheard of for couples who believed themselves infertile to conceive spontaneously when they'd given up all hope of having a child, but Katherine wished Liz had written to tell her.

It had been a long time since she'd heard from Poppy's adoptive mother. Not since a year ago when Poppy had turned sixteen and Liz had emailed Katherine, telling her that any further contact would be up to Poppy. In the meantime, if Katherine chose to continue writing, not emailing if she didn't mind as Liz couldn't monitor those, she would keep the letters but only pass them on to Poppy when and if she asked.

It hadn't been written to hurt her, although it had. In her heart, Katherine had wanted to argue but in her head she'd agreed. At sixteen Poppy was old enough to decide for herself whether she wanted to stay in touch. Katherine had always hoped that she would decide to—but not like this.

'I didn't know they had another child,' Katherine said. 'That must have been a surprise.'

'They didn't have *another* child. They had a child. I'm not their child. Not any longer. What is it with you lot that you can cast off your children when it suits you?'

'They put you out?' Katherine said, astonished and outraged. 'But that's—'

Poppy stared down at the floor. 'They didn't *exactly* put me out,' she mumbled. 'I mean, they never said in so many words that they wanted me to go—but it was obvious.'

'And they don't know where you are?' Katherine asked, beginning to recover. 'They'll be frantic You need to let your parents—'

'They're not my parents!'

'According to the law, they are. They've probably alerted the police. How did you leave without them knowing? *When* did you leave?'

'Yesterday morning. I said I was going to a sleepover at my friend Susan's'

Katherine was aghast. 'You *lied* to them?'

'Well, I could hardly tell them where I was going, could I?'

'If you're so convinced they don't care, why didn't you try it?' Katherine winced at the tone of her own voice. Now she sounded as snarky as her daughter.

Poppy glowered. 'They have to pretend, don't they, that they care? Even if it's all a big, fat act.'

'Of course they care and they need to know where you are. They need to know you're safe.'

'I don't want to talk to them.'

Katherine retrieved her mobile from her bag and held it out. 'Phone them. Now.'

'No.'

Katherine was tempted for a miniscule moment not to phone Liz and Mike. They might phone the police to return Poppy or at the very least insist Katherine put her on the next plane and she couldn't bear not to steal a day or two with her child. Her child! She gave herself a mental shake. Of course she couldn't possibly do that to Mike and Liz.

'You can't stay here unless you do. I'll have to notify the police.'

Poppy got up from the sofa and picked up her rucksack. 'In that case, I'm off. I should have known you wouldn't want me either. Jeez, I'm so stupid. You got rid of me once. Why on earth would you want anything to do with me now? I just thought you might have a little leftover maternal feeling—if not a sense that you owe me something at least.'

Katherine knew she was being manipulated, but even so, she couldn't let Poppy leave. Not now, not like this. If Poppy walked out her life, would she ever get another chance with her again? And under the sullen exterior Katherine glimpsed the lonely, confused child within. It took all her resolve not to march across the room and envelop her daughter in her arms. Somehow, instinctively, she knew that wasn't the way to handle the situation either. Best to remain calm and reasonable. After all, there must be *some* reason for Poppy to have sought her out—even if part of her motive was to hurt her adoptive parents as much as possible. She had to tread carefully.

'Poppy, please. I don't want you to go, that's not what I meant. I can't tell you how...' her heart swelled '...thrilled and delighted I am to see you.' She gestured towards the sofa. 'Please, sit back down. Let me phone your parents, talk to them. I'll ask if you can stay here for a couple of days. It'll give us a chance to talk...'

Katherine held her breath, her heart beating

in her throat, while Poppy considered what she'd said. Now that Poppy was here—here! In front of her! she couldn't bear not to grab this chance to talk to her, maybe hold her…even once.

Just when she thought her daughter was going to bolt for the door, she dropped her bag again.

'Okay.'

Relief made her legs weak. 'Great.'

'But I'm not going back. Ever.'

'We'll talk about it later.' Katherine sat down then stood up again. 'Look, why don't you have a shower—freshen up while I phone Liz and Mike? Then I'll make us something to eat, okay?'

Poppy's contemplated her from under her fringe for a few moments before nodding sullenly.

'I could do with a shower,' she admitted. 'I feel as if I've been in a sauna with my clothes on.' Now that she mentioned it, they did have a faint whiff of body odour. 'Then after that I could do with crashing. Is there a spare bedroom?'

'Yes. Let me get you some towels for your shower and check that the bed's made up.'

'Towels would be good, thanks. I don't think I brought one.'

Katherine hid a smile. It seemed that Poppy

had forgotten to forget her manners. And as if she'd realised the same thing, the scowl returned with a vengeance. 'No need to make the bed if its not already. I'm so bushed I could sleep in a pig's pen.'

As soon as she heard the shower running, Katherine dug her diary out of her handbag. She could still hardly believe that Poppy was here. And wanting to stay. It was what she'd always wished for, but in her imagination it had been organised in advance and arranged to perfection. Fear, excitement, nerves—a whole tumult of emotions coursed through her. But first things first: she had to let Poppy's parents know she was safe and well. Flicking through the pages until she found Mike and Liz's number, she sat down on the sofa and rested the phone on her lap. Twice she had to stop pressing the numbers her fingers were shaking so much.

'Poppy?' Liz sounded harassed and hopeful when she answered the phone. Katherine could hear an infant crying in the background. That had to be Charlie.

'No, it's Katherine.' It had been years since they'd spoken, all subsequent communication after the adoption having taken place by letter or email. 'But Poppy is here. Don't worry, she's fine.'

'Katherine? You say Poppy's with you? Thank God!' Liz started to cry. Katherine waited until she was able to speak. 'We've been beside ourselves. We didn't even know if she was alive. She just upped and disappeared. We thought… Oh, God. She's with you? And definitely all right?'

'She's a little travel weary. Nothing a sleep won't put right.' It was clear that whatever Poppy believed, Liz did care about her.

'Where are you?' Liz continued. 'We'll come and get her.'

'I'm in Greece. Working.'

'Greece? Poppy's in Greece?'

'She found me through my work email.' Katherine lowered her voice and glanced behind her to make sure Poppy hadn't suddenly come into the room. However she could still hear the sound of the shower running.

'She did? Mind you, she's a bright girl—almost too bright for her own good. That's why I wanted her to go to university, but she's not been working… I don't know if she's going to pass her A-levels. She's been going out till all hours despite being grounded and refusing to study. She's changed!'

Katherine smiled wryly.

'I gather you've had a baby. She seems upset about that.'

'Charlie? Oh, I know I've been caught up in caring for him. He's such a demanding baby. Not like Poppy at the same age. That doesn't mean we don't care about her, Katherine. We love her. She's our daughter!'

Katherine winced inwardly. As if she needed to be reminded. Liz broke down again.

'Should we come? No, I can't. Not with the baby—I haven't got around to getting a passport for him...Mike's working... I...' Liz said between sobs.

'She can stay with me for as long as she likes.'

'Oh, that would be a relief. She'd be all right with you.'

They finished the phone call with Katherine promising to keep Liz and Mike informed and also promising to try and convince Poppy to go home if she could. The problem was, Katherine didn't want her to go.

As she waited for Poppy to re-emerge, Katherine quickly laid the patio table and stood back to survey the results. She cocked a critical eye at the little vase of flowers she'd placed in the centre and hesitated. Too much? Definitely. Hastily she snapped it away but now the plain white tablecloth appeared too plain and unwelcoming so she placed the vase back. For God's sake, she was more nervous than on a first date—but this was way more important than that. Even with this little gesture she wanted Poppy to know how much she cared.

Hurrying back to the kitchen, she tossed the big bowl of salad and added a touch more seasoning. Was it too salty now? Did Poppy even like salt? Or figs, for that matter? Fish? Was she vegetarian, a vegan? She knew absolutely nothing about her, nothing. Not one single iota about her likes and dislikes. Well, perhaps a simple lunch was the place to find out.

The sound of the shower finally stopped. Nervously Katherine paced the small living room, preparing herself for Poppy's reappearance. *Keep conversation light and simple. Ask questions without probing. Get her trust.*

When the front door opened and Alexander walked in, Katherine could only stand and stare at him. With Poppy's sudden arrival, she'd completely forgotten they'd arranged to go out for lunch.

He strode into the room and gathered her into his arms, kissing her softly on the lips. 'I've missed you.' His eye caught the laid-out table. 'Oh, are we eating in, then?' He grinned. 'Smart thinking. I have to go and visit a patient later, but I have an hour or two before I need to leave—'

Katherine wriggled out his arms. 'Alexander, something's come up… Could we step outside a minute? There's something I have to tell you.'

He raised an eyebrow. 'Sounds ominous.' He studied her more closely. 'What is it? Something's really upsetting you. Have there been more meningitis cases reported?'

'No. It's not that.' She took him by the arm. 'We can't talk here.

'Hi. Are you her boyfriend?' Katherine whirled around to find Poppy, wearing only a skimpy towel, draped against the stairpost. When Katherine looked back at Alexander his eyebrows had shot even higher.

'I'm Alexander Dimitriou,' he replied, 'and you are?'

'Hasn't she told you? Well, that doesn't surprise me.' Poppy flounced into the room and sprawled on the sofa, her long thin, legs stretched in front of her. 'I'm Poppy.' She pointed at Katherine. 'And she's my mother. Or should I say the woman who gave birth to me. Not the same thing at all, is it?'

It was one of those moments when the room seemed to take a breath. Behind her scowl,

Poppy seemed pretty pleased with herself. Unsurprisingly, Alexander appeared bewildered, and as for her, it felt as if her legs were going to give way.

'Would you excuse us for a moment?' she said to Poppy. 'Alexander, could we speak outside for a moment?'

Still looking stunned, he followed her downstairs and out to the patio. She closed the door behind them.

'You have a daughter?' he said.

'Yes.'

'You have a daughter,' he repeated, with a shake of his head. 'You have a child and you didn't even mention her. Why the hell not?'

'I was going to tell you about her.'

'When?'

Good question. She had no answers right now. At least, none that would make sense to him.

'I didn't know she was coming.'

'Evidently,' he said dryly, folding his arms.

'I probably should have told you before now.'

He continued to hold her gaze. 'Probably. So where has she been all this time? Most women would mention they had a child and if I remember correctly you told me you were childless.'

'Oh, for heaven's sake,' she burst out, immediately on the defensive. 'It's not as if we—

I mean…' What the hell *did* she mean? She couldn't think straight. 'It's not as if we made promises…' Damn, that wasn't right either.

His mouth settled into a hard line. 'Fool that I am, I thought we did have something. I thought it was the beginning.'

Had he? He'd never said. But she couldn't think about that now. Not when Poppy was upstairs, waiting for her. She glanced behind her, caught between the need to return to her child and the need to talk to Alexander. Right now her child had to take precedence. Explanations would have to wait.

'Can we talk about this later?' she pleaded. 'I could come down to the bay.'

He shook his head. 'I think you've just made it clear that you don't owe me an explanation and I doubt there is anything…'

Poppy chose that moment to appear from the house, wearing a bikini and a towel slung casually over her shoulder.

'I'm going for a swim,' she said. 'Where's the coolest place to go?'

'Coolest?' Katherine echoed.

'Where the boys hang out. You don't think I'm going to hang out with you all the time, do you?'

'The little bay just below the house is quite

safe to swim in as long as you don't go too far out. Actually, perhaps it's better if you wait until I come with you before you go into the water. And if you're sunbathing, put factor thirty on. The sun here is stronger than you think.'

'I'm seventeen, not seven, you know. Besides, don't you think it's a bit late to do the maternal thing?'

Katherine winced. 'I've spoken to your mother. She knows you're with me. She's been worried about you.'

A faint gleam appeared in Poppy's eyes, to be replaced almost immediately by her habitual scowl. 'Serves them right.'

Katherine sneaked a look at Alexander. He looked confused. No wonder. 'Her mother?' She saw the dawning realisation in his eyes.

'Liz wants you to go home. They miss you,' she told Poppy.

'Well, I'm not going.' Poppy pouted. 'I always fancied a holiday in Greece.'

'We need to talk about that.'

'Whatever.' Poppy yawned, exposing her tongue and, to Katherine's horror, another piercing. She hid a shudder.

'I should go,' Alexander said stiffly.

Poppy sauntered past them and towards the bay. Katherine turned back to Alexander. 'I'll see you later. Or tomorrow. I'll explain everything then—'

'As I said, you don't owe me an explanation. Hadn't you better go after your daughter?'

'I had to give her up,' she said quickly.

'Did you?' he said coldly. And with that, he turned on his heel.

Alexander left Katherine standing on her patio and strode towards his car. He was stunned. How come she'd never mentioned that she had a child? How old was Poppy anyway? At least seventeen. So Katherine must have been around the same age when she'd had her. Had she been too dead set on a career in medicine to contemplate keeping a baby? If so, he'd had a narrow escape. Thank God he'd found out before he'd proposed. He'd never understand how a woman could give up her child.

But what he found harder to forgive was why she hadn't told him about her. He'd been open and honest with Katherine—sharing stuff that he'd never shared with anyone before—and she'd flung his honesty in his face. He'd let himself believe that finally he'd met a woman who matched up to Sophia, but he'd been mistaken. He'd thought she was pretty damn near perfect. What a fool he'd been. What a bloody fool. He'd come damn close to asking this woman—or at least the woman he'd thought she was—to spend the rest of her life with him. How could have believed he'd find someone as true as Sophia?

He wrenched his car door open with such force it banged against its hinges. Damn.

If Katherine thought that the evening would be spent chatting with her daughter she soon found she was mistaken. Every time she went near Poppy she'd pick up her book and walk away, and, after only picking at her supper she'd excused herself and gone to bed, slamming the door behind her. Left alone, and feeling raw, Katherine had pulled out her photograph album and picked out the photo of Poppy that had been taken on the beach.

What would her life have been like if she hadn't relinquished the care of her daughter to someone else? She would have been the one holding her. She would have been the recipient of those ice-cream kisses. It was something she would never know, although she had questioned it then, when her tiny infant had been gently but firmly tugged from her arms, and she wondered more than ever now.

Early the next morning while Poppy was still asleep Katherine sent a text to Alexander asking him to meet her down on the beach around the corner from her house. She didn't want to go to his home and she didn't want him to come to hers. Not when they could be overheard at either. Whatever he said she owed him an explanation.

He replied almost immediately, saying that he'd be there in five minutes. She tied her hair into a ponytail and applied a touch of lipstick and let herself out of the house.

She was sitting on a rock when he appeared. Her heart jerked when she saw the grim expression on his face. What else had she expected? She *had* lied to him.

'I don't have long,' he said, stopping in front of her, his hands thrust into the pockets of his light cotton trousers.

She leaped to her feet, hating the way he towered over her, making her feel a little like a schoolgirl waiting to be told off by the schoolmaster. 'Thank you for coming,' she said stiffly.

'Look,' he said, 'I can see you have a lot going on at the moment. What we had was fun but as you pointed out, it was never going to be anything but short term, was it? You have your life...' he glanced towards her house '...back in Britain and I have mine here.'

He'd clearly made up his mind about them,

then. She'd thought that after a night to think things over, he'd at the very least be prepared to listen to what she had to say.

'No,' she said softly. 'I can see that now. I came here to explain but if that's the way you feel…' She didn't wait for a response but, blinking back tears, turned back towards home—and Poppy.

Katherine paused outside her door and waited until she had her emotions under control before going inside. She gasped. It looked as if a tornado had hit it. There were empty cups and plates and a cereal carton scattered over the work surface. A damp towel was in a heap on the floor, along with several magazines. Her daughter's bedroom was in a worse state. Poppy's rucksack lay on her bed, clothes spilling from it, some on the floor. Instinctively Katherine began to pick up, folding the clothes as she went along.

She called out Poppy's name but there was no answer. She quickly searched the small villa and the garden, but there was no sign of her anywhere. Had she decided to go? But where? Back to Liz and Mike? Or somewhere else? It hadn't even crossed her mind that Poppy might up and leave. But if she had, wouldn't she have taken her rucksack? So where was she? Panic ripped through her. What if Poppy had ignored Katherine's warnings and had gone swimming and been dragged out to sea? She should never have left her alone. Underneath that sullen exterior was bound to be a desperately unhappy girl. Katherine had only just got her back and she'd failed her again.

She ran outside but there was no sign of her daughter. However, Alexander was still standing where she'd left him, apparently lost in thought.

She hurried over to him. 'I can't find her,' she said.

'Who? Poppy?'

'She's taken her swimming things but I looked—she's not in the bay.' She spread her arms wide. 'I can't see her anywhere.'

'I'll check the bay on the other side,' Alexander said. He squeezed her shoulder. 'Don't look so worried, she'll be fine.'

He couldn't know that for sure. She ran around to the bigger bay. On the small stretch of beach was another towel and a pair of sunglasses but no sign of Poppy.

She scanned the bay, searching for her, but apart from a couple of boats the sea was empty. A late-morning breeze had whipped it into frothy peaked waves. Had she gone for a swim and gone out too far?

'Where is she?' She grabbed Alexander's arm. 'We've got to find her.' She began tugging off her sandals.

'What the hell are you doing?'

'I'm going to swim out. I need to find her.'

Alexander gripped her by the shoulders. 'Calm down. Think about it. You'd see her if she's out there.' He cupped his hands and called out to one of the boats nearby. The man called back to him.

'He says he hasn't noticed a stranger, and he's been out here since dawn. He'll ask the other boats just to make sure. Come on, let's check the village. She's probably gone in search of a Coke. Someone will have seen her.

Filled with dread, Katherine followed him back up the steps. He stopped a woman and spoke to her in Greek. She shook her head. They asked several more people and they all denied seeing a young stranger. Katherine's panic was threatening to overwhelm her when the village store owner told them, his expression aghast, that, yes, he'd served a girl with short black hair and an earring in her lip. She was, he said, with Alexander's pretty daughter. The last was said with significantly more approval.

Inside Alexander's house, Grandmother was in her habitual place in the kitchen. In the small sitting room Crystal was lying on the sofa with her feet in Poppy's lap as Poppy painted her toenails. The little girl was giggling while Poppy seemed totally oblivious to the stir she'd caused. Katherine sagged with relief.

Then fury overtook her.

'Why the hell didn't you leave a note to say where you were?'

Poppy looked up in surprise. Immediately her face resumed its belligerent look. 'Why should I leave a note? You didn't and it's not as if you've ever known or cared what I do.'

'While you're staying with me, you're my responsibility. For God's sake, I thought you'd drowned. Your towel—all your things—were on the beach.'

Something shifted in Poppy's eyes. If Katherine hadn't known better she would have said it was regret.

'Well, as you can see, I haven't drowned. I went to the beach and came back to your house for a drink and Crystal turned up. She wanted some company.'

'Poppy's painting my toenails! See, Baba, she's made patterns on them.' When the child turned her face towards them, Katherine noticed that Poppy had also given her full make-up.

Alexander placed a restraining hand on Katherine's arm. 'Thanks for spending time with Crystal, Poppy.' He crossed the room and smiled down at his daughter. 'Have you seen my daughter, Crystal? She's a beautiful little girl with a clean, shining face who never needs make-up.'

Crystal glared at him. 'I am your daughter, silly. And I like my face the way Poppy has done it.'

Grandmother muttered something from behind Katherine. When she glanced at her she couldn't be sure whether it was amusement or disapproval on her face.

Alexander scooped Crystal into his arms. 'I think it's time for a wash.'

'But Poppy is going to do my fingernails next. Then we're going to get dressed up and go to the square.'

'Poppy, we need to go,' Katherine said firmly.

'Oh, all right.' She stood up. 'See you tomorrow, Crystal.'

'That woman is not good,' Alexander's grandmother told him when he returned from helping Crystal to dress. 'What kind of woman gives away her child? I am disappointed. I thought I had found the right woman for you.'

So Poppy hadn't wasted any time in telling Crystal and Grandmother her story. 'We shouldn't judge her, Yia-Yia. Not until we know her reasons.' But wasn't what she'd said exactly what he'd been thinking? Katherine clearly wasn't the woman he'd thought she was. No doubt she'd had her reasons for giving her daughter up for adoption—although he couldn't think what they could be. She'd lied about having a child—that's what he couldn't bring himself to forgive. He'd thought he knew her. Now he knew better.

But a few days later his heart kicked against his ribs when he saw her emerge from the village store.

She hurried along the street, a few steps in front of him, and he was appalled to find that the villagers no longer called out to her or smiled in her direction. Since Poppy had arrived the village had been alight with gossip about her and her mother. Word had it that Poppy had been abandoned as a baby—where, no one could say exactly, but it varied between a hospital doorstep and an alleyway, that she had been taken away from Katherine because

she had been unfit to look after her, to all sorts
of even crazier versions. One of the other ru-
mours he'd heard had involved Poppy running
away from adoptive parents who beat her to a
mother who hadn't wanted her in the first place.
It seemed now that they knew about Poppy and
having made up their minds, they had decided
to spurn Katherine. Alexander suspected that
most of the gossip had originated from Poppy,
who no doubt was making the most of the sympathy she was getting from the women in the
village.

He'd seen mother and daughter yesterday,
sitting on the downstairs patio. Both had been
wearing shorts, revealing long brown legs, both
barefoot. When they'd turned to look at him,
two identical pairs of blue eyes had stared out
from porcelain complexions. It was obvious
they were closely related, although, given the
gap in their ages, they might have been taken
for sisters rather than mother and daughter—
even with the radically different hairstyles and
Poppy's piercing.

Feeling she was being unfairly accused was
one thing, re-igniting their aborted love affair
quite another. Nevertheless, it was about time
the gossip stopped.

Furious with them, or himself—he couldn't

be sure which—he called Katherine's name and ran the few steps to catch up with her. He took the shopping bag from her hand. 'Let me carry this for you.'

She looked up at him, defiance shining in her blue eyes. 'I can manage,' she said. 'You don't have to keep the fallen woman company.'

But behind the defiance he could see the hurt and his chest tightened. No matter what she said, she'd been wounded badly by the villagers' attitude. She'd told him how much she'd loved feeling part of their small community.

'You'll be a seven-day wonder,' he said. 'Then they'll forget all about it.'

'I'm not so sure,' she said. 'But I won't be judged. Not by them—not by anyone.' She looked at him again. He knew she was including him in her statement and she was right. He had been as guilty as the rest of drawing conclusions without having the facts. 'Neither do I need you to stick up for me.'

'I know. You're perfectly able to do that yourself.' He was rewarded by the briefest of smiles.

'How is the prodigal daughter anyway?' he asked. 'I understand she spends a fair bit of time at my house.'

'She seems to get a kick out of being around your grandmother. She's shown her how to make soap from olive oil, how to dry herbs and how to cook. The things she was showing me before I fell out of favour. Don't get me wrong, I'm sure she's wonderfully patient with her and I'm happy Poppy has someone she feels good around.'

'She tells me Poppy is very good at entertaining Crystal. I suspect my grandmother sees a different side to Poppy than you do.'

She smiled sadly. 'I'm trying to get to know her. I'm trying not to nag, just to make her aware that I'm ready to talk whenever she's ready. I thought that she would have begun to unbend towards me a bit, but she seems as angry with me as she was the day she arrived.' Her shoulders sagged and he had to ball his fists to stop himself taking her in his arms.

'Give her time. She hasn't gone home so being here must mean something to her.'

'I don't think I'm anything more than a bolt-hole to her. And in many ways I'm glad just to be that. I took her to Mycenae the other day. I thought doing things together would help us to bond.' She laughed bitterly. 'I was wrong. It was nothing short of a disaster. She managed half an hour before she sulked off back to the car.'

Despite everything, he had to suppress a smile. 'You know the ruins of ancient cities aren't everyone's cup of tea. Especially when they're teens. From what little I know of Poppy she strikes me as more of a beach girl.'

'But I thought she'd be interested—I would have been at her age. I thought we'd have something to talk about at least. Something that was less emotional than our relationship and what's going on with her back home.'

She looked so disappointed he almost reached out for her. Instead, he dug his hands even deeper into his pockets. But was she really so naïve to think that dragging a seventeen-year-old around ruins was the way build a relationship?

'Have you asked her what *she* wants to do?'

'Of course! I'm not a complete idiot.'

'And her answer?'

'Let me use her exact words. "Duh. To chill."'

Alexander hid another smile. She'd mimicked the little he'd heard of Poppy's truculent voice exactly. 'Then just let her to do whatever she wants. If that means hanging around my grandmother's or sunbathing on the balcony or beach, just let her. She'll come to you when she's ready.'

'I've tried. But every time I go near her she gets up and walks away.' Her blue eyes were bewildered.

'Tell you what,' he found himself saying. 'There's some caves with amazing stalactites and stalagmites not very far from here. And there's a good beach nearby—shallow, so it's great for swimming—so why don't the four of us go there tomorrow?'

'You must have other things you want to do.' But he could tell by the way her eyes lit up that she liked the idea. She looked like a drowning woman being tossed a float. He hadn't planned to suggest a trip together, but the words were out and he couldn't take them back. Not that he wanted to take them back. A day with Katherine was suddenly irresistible.

'Crystal would like nothing better than to spend the day with her new idol—especially if it involves a boat trip in caves followed by a picnic and a swim. No, I promise you that is my daughter's idea of a dream day and so it's mine too. Do you want me to ask Poppy?'

'I'll do it,' she said, taking her shopping from him. Suddenly she stood on tiptoe and kissed him on the cheek. 'Thank you,' she said.

To Katherine's surprise, when she told Poppy the next morning about Alexander's invitation, she seemed keen to go. She disappeared into the shower and returned an hour later dressed and carrying one of Katherine's bags. In the meantime, Katherine had prepared a picnic with some of the fresh bread she'd bought from the village store as soon as it had opened. She'd also made a fig and mozzarella salad, which she'd put in a plastic container. There were olives, cold meat, soft drinks, and crisps too. She hoped Poppy would find at least some of it to her taste. As she made her preparations her head buzzed. Did Alexander's invite mean he was ready to listen to her? Or was he simply sorry for her? Whatever the reason, she had to at least try and make him understand.

Crystal ran into the room ahead of her father. 'We are going to swim. We're going to see magic caves! And you are coming too.'

'Yeah,' Poppy said, sliding a look at Katherine. 'So she says.' Then her daughter's face broke into a wide smile and picked Crystal up. 'Let's get into the car.'

Alexander looked as gorgeous as ever in a pair of faded jeans and a white T-shirt and Katherine's heart gave an uncomfortable thump. She couldn't read the expression in his eyes when they rested on her. Perhaps at a different time they might have had something—perhaps if she'd been a different person... Timing had never been her strong suit.

'Ready?' he asked.

'As I'll ever be.'

Crystal did all the talking as they drove towards the caves. 'I can swim, you know,' she told Poppy proudly. 'Can you?'

'Of course,' Poppy replied. 'I swim for my school.'

Katherine was surprised. But delighted. They had this in common at least. 'I swam for my school too,' she remarked.

'Whatever.'

Katherine shared a look with Alexander. It would take time, it seemed, for Poppy to unbend towards her—if she ever did.

They parked at the top car park and, leaving their bags and the picnic, walked the rest of the way. The sky was a brilliant blue, feathered with the slightest clouds, and the sea was turquoise against the blindingly white shore.

They bought the tickets for the boat trip into the caves and the children were given life jackets to put on. Poppy looked as if she was about to refuse but clearly thought better of it. Katherine was relieved. No doubt if she had refused, Crystal would have too.

The girls clambered into the front of the boat, with Katherine and Alexander squashed

together on one of the seats in the stern. She
was painfully aware of the familiar scent of the
soap he used and the pressure of his leg against
hers. She closed her eyes, remembering the feel
of his arms around her, the way her body fit-
ted perfectly against his, the way he made her
laugh. She shook the images away. They might
never be lovers again, but did him being here
now mean that at the very least he was still her
friend?

As their guide used an oar to push the boat
further into the depths of the caves she gasped.
Thousands of spectacular stalactites hung from
the roof of the cave, which was lit with small
lights that danced off the crystal formations like
thousands of sparks.

Crystal turned around, eyes wide, her small
hands covering her mouth. 'It is a magic cave,
Baba. It's like Christmas! Only better!'

Even Poppy seemed stunned by their beauty.
She spent the trip with her arm around Crystal's shoulders, pointing out different formations. Katherine had read about them yesterday
after Alexander had extended his invitation and
was able to tell the girls how they'd been formed
as well as a little history of the caves. Poppy
asked some questions, appearing to have forgotten that she wasn't speaking to Katherine.

Katherine glanced at Alexander and he grinned back. He'd been right. This was the kind of trip to impress a seventeen-year-old—inasmuch as *anything* could impress this particular seventeen-year-old.

Their trip into the caves finished, Alexander returned to the car for their costumes and their picnic, while Katherine and the girls found a spot on the grass, just above the pebbly beach, where they could lay their picnic blanket. As soon as Alexander came back Poppy and Crystal disappeared off to the changing rooms to put on their swimming costumes.

'Aren't you going to swim?' Alexander asked.

'In a bit. What about you?'

'What are the chances of Crystal letting me just lie here?' When he grinned she could almost make herself believe that they were still together.

The girls came out of the changing rooms and ran down into the sea, squealing as the water splashed over their knees.

'She's a good kid,' Alexander said.

'Yes. I believe she is.'

'What happened to her father?'

Katherine sighed. It was a question she'd been waiting for Poppy to ask. 'Ben? Last time

I heard, he was married with three children and doing very well as a lawyer.'

'You must have been very young when you had her.'

'I was seventeen. Sixteen when I fell pregnant.'

'You don't have to tell me anything you don't want to. It's none of my business.'

'No,' she said. 'I'd like to. It's not something I've ever spoken to anyone about, but I think I owe it to you to tell you the truth.'

'I don't want you to tell me because you think you owe me, although I would like to understand. It's not so much that you have a child you gave up for adoption, it's the fact you didn't tell me. Hell, Katherine, I bared my soul to you.'

'I know...' She sighed. 'It's just—it's been a secret I've kept for so long, afraid of what people would think if they knew...'

'I can't imagine the Katherine I know caring about what people think.'

'We all care what people think if we're honest—at least, the opinions of those we love and respect.'

'If they love and respect us, then their feelings shouldn't change...' he said slowly. He was quiet for a long time. 'I promise I'll listen this time.'

'It's a long story.'

He nodded in the direction of the girls, who were splashing each other and laughing. 'Looks like they're not going to be out of the water any time soon.'

Seeing Poppy like this reminded Katherine how painfully young her daughter still was and how painfully young she herself had been when she'd fallen pregnant. A child really.

'Remember I told you that I won a scholarship to high school?'

He nodded.

'I was proud and excited to have won it but I was totally unprepared for the reality. Being there terrified me. Most of the rest of the pupils came from well-to-do families—the children of business people, doctors and lawyers. I was desperately shy as it was, and with my second-hand uniform I knew I stuck out. Unsurprisingly perhaps, they wanted nothing to do with me. I pretended I didn't care. At break times I'd take a book and read it. I knew I still had to get top marks if I wanted to be accepted at medical school.

'I was in my second year when I met Ben. I'd been roped in to swim for the school team in the swimming gala—it was the one sport I seemed naturally good at—and he was there. He was a couple of years older than me, as confident as I was shy, as good-looking as I was geeky—but for some reason he seemed to like me.

'We were friends at first. We spent our break times together, usually in the library or just walking around, talking about history and politics—even then he knew he wanted to be a lawyer—stuff that no one else was interested in discussing but that we both loved to debate.

'Being Ben's friend changed everything. I wasn't lonely any more. I now realised there were people just like me who didn't care about clothes and the latest hairstyle. Then when I was in fourth year and he was in sixth year—he already had a place to read law—everything changed and we became boyfriend and girlfriend. He'd come around to my house. By that time Mum and Dad had bought a small restaurant and were working all hours to get it established, but then Dad died suddenly. Mum, as you can imagine, was devastated and so was I. I clung to Ben and eventually the inevitable happened. We slept together.

'It didn't seem wrong—quite the opposite. It seemed a natural progression. We'd talked often about how, when he was a lawyer—famous and defending the poor and downtrodden, of course—and I was a doctor, the very best, of course...' she risked a smile in Alexander's direction, and was reassured to find he was looking at her with the same intent expression he always had when they talked '…saving lives and discovering new treatments and cures, we'd marry and have a family. But then I fell pregnant. Stupid, I know. We did use contraception but with the optimism and ignorance of youth we weren't as careful as we should have been.

'By that time, he was about to leave to start his law degree and I had just sat my A-levels. I expected, rightly as it turned out, to get all As and I was confident I would get a place in medical school.

'To say we were both shellshocked would be an understatement. We talked about getting married, but we couldn't see how. My parents' restaurant was struggling without Dad and barely making enough for Mum to live on, and she'd been recently diagnosed with multiple sclerosis. Ben's parents weren't much better off. There didn't seem any way to have the baby.'

'What about Ben? Didn't he have a say?'

'Terminating the pregnancy was Ben's preferred option.' She looked over to where Crystal and Poppy were splashing each other and her heart stuttered. Thank God she'd never seriously considered it. 'He said he couldn't see a way of supporting me or our baby—he still desperately wanted to be a lawyer—and one night he told me that if I continued with the pregnancy he couldn't be part of either of our lives.

'We broke up. With the pregnancy something had changed between us. It was as if all that had gone on before had just been us play-acting at being a couple. Maybe if we were older... Whatever, I couldn't blame him. I didn't want to marry him, I knew that then—just as I knew I wasn't ready to be a mother. But neither could I bear to terminate the pregnancy. Oh, I thought about it. I even went as far as making an appointment with the hospital, but when it came down to it I just couldn't go through with it. I knew then I had to tell my mother. It was the most difficult conversation I've ever had in my life. I could see her imagining her and Dad's dreams of a better life for me going down the plughole. She lost it and broke down.

'When she'd pulled herself together she said that she would look after the child. It would mean my delaying going to university for a year but we'd manage. Just as we always had. But she was ill—some days I had to help her get dressed—and even then I knew what a diagnosis of MS meant. I knew she couldn't help take care of a child—not when she would need more and more care herself. I was in a bad way,

Alexander. I felt so alone.' She took a shuddering breath.

'I told her that I had decided to have the baby but that I was going to give it up for adoption. I'd done my research, you see. I knew that you could arrange an open adoption. I would get to pick the parents—ones already pre-selected by the adoption agency. My child would always know they were adopted, and although I could never see him or her, I could write care of the adoptive parents and in return they would send me updates. If I couldn't keep the baby myself, it seemed the only—the best—solution.

'My mother tried to argue me out of it—she couldn't imagine how any child of hers could even consider giving their child away, and I think she believed I would change my mind.

'But she was wrong. I refused to imagine it as a baby. Instead, I pored over the biographies of the would-be adoptive parents. The adoption agency did a thorough job. There were photographs, bits of information about their extended families, letters from them. It was heart-breaking, reading their stories. I could almost hear their desperation. They had to advertise themselves to me—they had to make me want to pick them.

'When I read about these couples I knew I

was doing the right thing. At least I managed to convince myself that I was. Far better for the child I was carrying to have a home with a couple who would be able to give them the love and attention I couldn't. In the end I picked out one family. They weren't particularly well off—I wasn't so naïve that I thought money was all that important—but they were financially secure. Enough to give my child everything he or she could ever need.

'But more than that, it was them as people who made them shine. They seemed kind, loving and so desperate to have afamily to shower love on. They'd been trying for a baby for several years and were getting close to the age where they'd no longer be able to put themselves forward for adoption. This was, I knew, their final chance of having a child. They also said that they hoped, in time, to adopt an older child, a brother or sister for this one. I liked that. I didn't want my child to grow up, like I did, as an only child. I wanted him or her to have a sibling who would always be there for them. So I picked them. I could have picked any of a dozen couples but I picked them.

'I know you probably can't imagine how anyone could do what I did. But I thought, I really believed I was doing the best thing for her. I insisted on an open adoption—I wouldn't have chosen Mike and Liz if they hadn't agreed to that—because although I couldn't keep Poppy myself I wanted to know that wherever she was in the world she was all right.

'But Mum was right. I hadn't accounted for how I would feel as my pregnancy continued. I began to feel protective of this child growing inside me. I didn't know what to do. I had already committed to giving her up and I knew her prospective parents were longing to welcome her into her family. But even then I thought about changing my mind—even though I knew the grief it would cause them and even though I knew I was too young to bring up a child. I began to persuade myself that with Mum's help we would manage.'

She paused and looked out to sea. 'But then Mum's multiple sclerosis returned with a vengeance. She had to have a wheelchair and she couldn't do even the basics for herself. I wondered if the stress of my pregnancy had made her worse. I felt as if it was all my fault. I didn't know what to do. So in the end I kept to my original decision and gave her up.

'The day I gave birth to her was one of the worst in my life. The labour was easy compared to what came next. They allowed me a few hours alone with her to say my goodbyes. I hadn't realised how difficult it would be. Here was this tiny thing in my arms, looking up at me as if I was the only thing in her world. I felt such an overwhelming love for her it shook me to the core. But how could I go back on my decision then? I was only seventeen. I thought it was unfair to everyone if I did. So I let them take her from me.'

It was only when he leaned across and wiped the tears from her face with the pad of his thumb that she realised she was crying. He waited without saying anything until she'd regained control again.

'I wrote to Liz often and she wrote back, telling me about Poppy's progress and sending photos. I knew when her baby teeth fell out, I knew when she got chickenpox, I saw her in her school uniform on her first day at school. I had more regrets then   seeing the photos of her, watching her grow up, albeit from a distance, made her real in a way she hadn't been before. Of course, by then it was too late to get her back. Mike and Liz were her parents and there was no doubt they loved her and that she loved them.'

He said nothing, just waited until she was ready to continue.

'I sailed through my final year at school and all my exams at medical school. But I worked for it. I hardly went out, hardly joined any clubs or societies, just worked. It all had to be for something, you see? If I'd failed I don't think I could have lived with myself. Mum never spoke of it. It was as if we pretended it hadn't happened. But sometimes I'd see Mum looking at me with such sadness it ripped me in two. I caught her once. About six months after I'd had Poppy. She was in the small bedroom at the front, the one that we kept for visitors. She was kneeling on the floor with a pile of baby clothes in front of her. She was smoothing out each item with her palms, murmuring to herself, before she placed it in a little box. Tears were running down her face. I doubt she even knew she was crying. You see the adoption only became final after six months. I could have changed my mind up until then and, believe me, sometimes I thought I might. But when I thought of the couple who had Poppy, how happy they'd been, I knew I had done the right thing. But I know now that Mum always hoped I would change my mind.

'She didn't see me so I tiptoed away. What was the point in saying anything? Even if I'd wanted to it was too late to change my mind. I had to keep believing I'd done the right thing.

'We never spoke about it. Not once.'

She drew in a shuddering breath. 'By all accounts, she was a happy child. She grew up knowing that she was adopted—that was part of the deal—and I guess it was just something she accepted.

'So many times I wished I could have been there to hold her when she was sick, to hear her laughter, just see her.' She swallowed the lump that had come to her throat. 'But I knew I had given away all my rights. I was just pleased to be allowed into her life—if only in small slices.'

'And have you told her this?'

'I've tried. But every time I raise the topic, she gets up and walks away.'

'Yet she came to find you.'

'I'm not sure she came to find me for the right reasons. When Poppy turned sixteen, Liz said that she would no longer give her my letters unless she asked. She also said that she wouldn't pass on news of Poppy. She thought, at sixteen, Poppy had the right to decide what place, if any, I had in her life. I heard nothing after that. It seemed Poppy had made her decision and I couldn't blame her. I hoped when she was older that she might seek me out.' She laughed shortly. 'I just never imagined it would be now.'

'What made her come to find you?'

'I think it was the new baby. Liz and Mike didn't think they could have children—that's why they decided to adopt. I know they intended to adopt another child, but they never did. About eighteen months ago, Liz fell pregnant—as you know, it can happen long after a couple has given up hope. The child is eight months now. I suspect Poppy's nose has been put out of joint. A baby can be demanding and she's bound to feel a little pushed out. Liz also said she's been bunking off school and her grades have taken a turn for the worse. If she carries on like this then there will be no chance of her getting accepted at university.'

'And that's important to you and to Liz?'

'Yes. Of course. Wouldn't you want the same for Crystal?'

'I want Crystal to be happy. I found out the hard way that success at work isn't the same as having success in life. Nothing is more important than being with your family. Nothing is more important than their happiness. At least to me.'

She felt stung. Somehow she'd hoped that she could make him understand, but it appeared she'd been mistaken. She bent over and undid her sandals. 'I've told you everything. Now I'm going to join the children in the water.'

Alexander watched her tiptoe gingerly into the sea. Her legs had browned in the sun and appeared to go on for ever in the tiny shorts she was wearing. He cursed himself inwardly. She was right. Who was he to judge her? It wasn't as if he had nothing to regret. But he'd wanted her to be perfect—which was rich, given that he was anything but. He still loved her but he needed time to get used to this different version of the Katherine he'd thought he'd known.

'Baba!' Crystal called from the water. 'Come in!' He rolled up the bottoms of his jeans, pulled his T-shirt over his head and went to join them.

It was, Katherine had to admit, despite the tension between her and Poppy and her and Alexander, a happy day—one of the happiest of her life. Despite everything how couldn't it be when she was spending it with the people she loved most? They swam and ate, then swam some more. As the afternoon became cooler, Alexander bought some fish from a boat he swam out to and they built a small fire over which they roasted the fish.

By the time they drove home, Crystal and Poppy were flushed with tiredness and happiness. Poppy had even come to sit next to Katherine when Alexander had taken Crystal away to dry her off and help her change back into her clothes.

'It's cool here,' Poppy said. 'I think I'd like to stay until you go back. If that's all right with you?'

'Of course,' Katherine said, delighted. 'Until I go back at the end of the month, at any rate. Will you let your mother know?'

'Sure,' Poppy said, and leaned back, hooking her arms behind her head. 'I kind of miss them. Even the crazy baby.'

'They miss you too.' She didn't want to say anything else, frightened of spoiling the fragile truce that had sprung up between them. There would be time to talk in the days to come. At the very least she owed it to Poppy to keep trying to explain why she'd given her up. Maybe Alexander was right. She shouldn't force it. Just tell Poppy she was happy to talk about it and leave it to her to bring it up when she was ready.

Back home, Alexander parked the car in the square and lifted Crystal into his arms. 'Perhaps we could do this again?' he said.

She looked at him. 'Maybe. I'm not sure.'

She still felt hurt. They had been friends before they'd become lovers. Didn't that count for anything?

He nodded and, holding his daughter in his arms, turned towards his house. Back home, Poppy also excused herself, saying she had her sleep to catch up on. Katherine suspected that she wanted to phone Liz in privacy and she was glad.

She poured herself a glass of wine and took it out onto the balcony. She'd told Alexander everything. At least now there were no more secrets between them.

She didn't see much of Alexander over the next few days, although Crystal and Poppy continued to visit each other's houses.

Katherine went to call Poppy for supper one day to find her up to her elbows in flour. 'I just want to finish these baklavas,' she said.

Alexander's grandmother looked at Katherine, shook her head and said something to Crystal in Greek. For one mortifying moment Katherine wondered if she was being told not to visit again, but to her surprise Crystal told her that her grandmother wanted her to come and sit with her outside on the bench by the front door.

Bemused, Katherine did as she asked.

They sat on the bench and Alexander's grandmother reached out and patted her hand. As people passed she kept her hand on Katherine's. Every time one of the villagers passed, her grip would tighten and she'd smile, while calling out a greeting. Many stopped and said a few words to Grandmother and greeted Katherine too, with a 'Hello' and 'How are you?'

So that was what the old lady was up to. Whatever she thought of Katherine's decision to give her child up for adoption, she was, in her own quiet way, telling the other villagers that she supported her. Tears burned behind Katherine's eyes. It was an unexpected, touching gesture from Grandmother and she wondered whether Alexander was behind it.

Speaking of which, he was coming across the square towards them. Katherine's heart leaped. Frightened he would see the desolation in her eyes, she lowered her lids until she was sure she could look at him calmly.

'Oh, hello.' He bent and kissed his grandmother on her cheek. He said something to her in Greek and she laughed. The old lady got to her feet and retreated back inside, leaving her space on the bench for Alexander.

'I think she had an ulterior motive for sitting

with me here,' Katherine murmured. 'I suspect she's telling the village to stop shunning me. Did you have anything to do with it?'

'No one tells Grandmother what to do, least of all me,' he said evasively. 'But I need to tell you, I've forgiven you for giving up Poppy. I'm sure you did what you had to and for the best possible motives.'

Katherine leaped to her feet. 'Forgiven me? Forgiven me! How dare you? I wanted your understanding, not your forgiveness. You're right about one thing. I should have told you earlier. That was wrong of me. But if you think I need forgiveness for giving birth to her then you are badly mistaken. And as for giving her away, you make it sound like tossing out so much rubbish. That's not the way I felt. I gave her to two loving, stable parents and it ripped me apart. You just need to spend time with her to know she's a young woman any parent would be proud of.'

Tears burned behind her eyes. She didn't even care that her outburst had garnered a bit of an audience. 'As far as I'm concerned,' she hissed, 'if I never see you again it will be too soon.' She whirled around to find Poppy standing behind her. Her daughter grinned. 'Way to go, Katherine. Way to go!'

* * *

Katherine and Poppy talked late into the night after Poppy had witnessed her outburst. It hadn't been an easy conversation—there had been no instant falling into each other's arms, but the tension and angst had begun to ease. There would, Katherine knew, be many more such conversations and bumpy roads but they had made a start. It would take time for them to be totally at ease with one another, but at least they were moving in that direction. And despite the rift between her and Alexander, she was more content than she had been in years.

'Crystal's great-grandmother isn't well,' Poppy told her a couple of days later. Katherine's heart tumbled inside her chest. She was deeply fond of the old lady but hadn't seen her since she'd made an absolute exhibition of herself by ranting at Alexander in public.

'Do you know what's wrong with her?'

'Crystal says she has a bad cold but she didn't get up this morning.'

If Grandmother had taken to her bed she had to be ill. 'Where is Crystal?'

'I left her at the house. I wanted her to come with me so I could tell you but she wouldn't leave Yia-Yia.'

Katherine snapped the lid of her laptop closed. 'Does Crystal's father know?'

'I don't think so.'

'Come on,' Katherine said, picking up the medical bag she'd brought with her. Luckily she had a whole case of antibiotics left over from the meningitis outbreak. Did Yia-Yia have a chest infection? If she did, it wasn't good. But she shouldn't get ahead of herself. It was possible Grandmother did have just a cold.

But as soon as she saw her she knew this was no ordinary cold. The old woman was flushed and clearly running a temperature.

'Poppy, could you take Crystal to our house, please? Stay there until I come for you. You can go down to the bay if you like but no further. Do you understand?'

Was it possible that the meningitis had come back in another form? No, that was unlikely if not impossible. However, until she knew for sure what it was, it was important to keep her away from the others.

For once Poppy didn't argue with her. She took Crystal by the hand. 'Go fetch your costume. My mum will look after your great-grandmother.'

It was the first time Poppy had called her Mum and a lump came to Katherine's throat.

She swallowed hard and made herself focus. She had a job to do.

After listening to Yia-Yia's chest and taking her temperature, which as she'd expected was way too high, Katherine phoned Alexander.

'I'll come straight away,' he said, when she told him.

'I'll give her oral antibiotics,' Katherine said, 'but she could do with them IV to be on the safe side. Do you want me to take her to hospital?'

'Wait until I get there,' he said. 'I'll be thirty minutes.'

While she waited for him to arrive, Katherine wetted a facecloth in cold water and wrung it out, before placing it on Grandmother's forehead. When the old lady tried to push her away she soothed her with a few words in Greek, grateful that it had improved to the point where she could reassure her.

'Alexander is on his way,' she said softly. 'He says you are to lie quietly and let me look after you until he gets here.'

'Crystal? Where is she?'

'Poppy has taken her to my house. Don't worry, she'll make sure she's all right.'

The elderly woman slumped back on her pillows, worryingly too tired to put up a fight.

Alexander must have driven as if the devil himself was behind him as he arrived in twenty minutes instead of the thirty he'd told her. He nodded to Katherine before crouching at his grandmother's side.

'Her pulse is around a hundred and shallow. She's pyrexial. I've given her antibiotics by mouth. Crystal is with Poppy. I thought it best.'

When Alexander looked up she could see the anguish in his eyes. He took out his stethoscope and Katherine helped Grandmother into a sitting position while Alexander listened to her chest again.

'As I thought. A nasty chest infection. She's probably caught a dose of the flu that's been going around and a secondary infection has set in very fast.'

'Does she need to go to hospital?'

Grandmother plucked at Alexander's sleeve. 'She says she won't go,' he translated. 'She wants to stay in her own home.'

'In that case,' Katherine said, 'that's what's going to happen. We can easily put her on a drip and give her IV antibiotics that way. Poppy and I can help look after her. What do you think?'

'I think it's risky.'

'More risky than admitting her to hospital?'

His shoulders slumped. 'You're right.'

She wished she could put her arms around him and tell him everything would be okay, but nothing in his demeanour suggested he would welcome the overture.

'I'll stay here with your grandmother,' Katherine said, 'while you fetch whatever it is we'll need.'

Later when they had Grandmother on a drip and her breathing was better, Katherine slipped home to ask Poppy to take Crystal back to her father. A short while later she was standing on the balcony when she became aware that Poppy had come to stand beside her. 'Is she going to get better?' she whispered.

'I hope so.' She reached out for her daughter's hand and squeezed it. Poppy didn't pull away. Instead, she leaned into her. Katherine pulled her close. 'We're all going to do everything to make sure she will. But, sweetheart, I think you should go back to Liz and Mike. If flu is going around, I don't want you to get it.'

'But I could have it already and just not be showing the symptoms yet. If I go back I could pass it on to my baby brother.' It was the first time she'd referred to Charlie as her baby brother. 'So I'm staying,' Poppy continued in a tone that sounded much like her own when she wouldn't be argued with. 'I'll help you look after Grandmother and any of the villagers who need help. I can't nurse them but I can cook and run errands.'

Katherine's eyes blurred as she considered her amazing child. 'I'm so proud of you,' she said. 'Did I ever tell you that?'

Poppy grinned back at her. 'And I'm proud of you. Now, shouldn't we get busy?'

'I think it's time I went home,' Poppy said. She'd been a godsend this last two weeks, helping by playing with Crystal while Alexander and Katherine took turns caring for Grandmother. They barely saw each other, the one leaving as the other took over. She'd also helped care for some of the other elderly villagers who'd fallen ill with flu. But Grandmother was much better, as were the others affected. 'I think Mum can do with some help with Charlie.' She looked at Katherine, a small frown between her brows. 'You're okay...' she grinned self-consciously '...but she's still my mum.'

'Of course she is. She's the woman who's cared for you all your life, the woman who nursed you through all your childhood sicknesses. Who was always there for you. Of course she'll always be your mum. But I hope you'll always remember that I love you too. If it helps, think of me as an honorary aunt. Someone who will always be there for you.'

'You know, and I don't mean this to sound horrible, I'm glad you gave me up. I can't imagine anyone except Liz and Mike being my parents. I mean, they get on my nerves sometimes but, you know, they've always been there.'

Katherine winced at the implied rebuke in Poppy's words.

'Would you still have given me away if you had the chance to do it all over again?'

Katherine took her time thinking about her answer. She loved Poppy too much to be anything less than honest.

'I feel so lucky that you are part of my life now—to have been given this second chance to get to know you. And knowing you now, I can't imagine a scenario where I would ever give you up. But back then I didn't know you and I wasn't the person I am now. Remember I was about your age. Half grown up and half still a child. Everything seemed so black and white then.

'I do know that I thought of you almost every day and receiving the updates about you from Liz were the highlight of my year. Wait there. I'd like to show you something.'

She went inside and retrieved the album she always carried with her. She placed it on the patio table. 'Liz sent me a photo of you on every birthday and Christmas. This is you on your first birthday.' She passed a photograph to Poppy. She was standing in front of a birthday cake with a single candle. A hand belonging to someone just out of shot was supporting her and Poppy was grinning into the camera, two small teeth showing. Katherine handed her several more photos. 'Here you are on your first day at school, when you joined the Brownies, your first swimming lesson, your first trip to the beach. Liz sent me a letter with every photograph and sometimes a little souvenir from your life—like this picture you drew when you came back from a holiday in Spain. I wrote to you too.

'I'm not pretending any of that makes up for not bringing you up myself, but I knew you were happy and so I could live with my decision.'

'Why didn't you ever get married?'

'The right person never came along. One of the things I promised myself when I gave you up was that I would concentrate on being the best doctor I could be.'

'And you did.' The admiration in her daughter's eyes made her want to cry.

'I'm human, Poppy. You of all people know that. Don't ever think anyone can be perfect.'

'You like Alexander, don't you?' Poppy said out of the blue. 'And I think he likes you too.'

It felt odd discussing her love life, or rather lack of it, with her seventeen-year-old daughter.

'He did once, I think.' She leaned across and wrapped her arms around her child. 'But I've got you now. And that's more than enough for me.'

Two days later, the tickets home were booked and Poppy had gone for a nap, exhausted after a day spent cooking and running errands. Her daughter was truly an amazing young woman.

Katherine had made supper but Poppy hadn't reappeared. She boiled the kettle and made her some of her favourite camomile tea. She loved how she now knew these small details about her child.

Taking the tea with her, she tiptoed into Poppy's bedroom. Her daughter was lying spreadeagled on the bed, the sheets tangled in her long limbs. Once more Katherine sent a silent prayer upwards for whatever had brought her daughter back to her.

But something about the way Poppy's face was screwed up—as if she were in pain—made her cross the room and place a hand on her child's forehead. At the feel of cold sweat alarm shot through her. Poppy had been complaining of a sore stomach the night before but this was something more.

Perhaps she had the same flu that had brought Grandmother and some of the other villagers low? Stamping down on the panic that threatened to overwhelm her, she gently shook her daughter by the shoulder. 'Poppy, wake up.'

Poppy opened her eyes, groaned and closed them again.

Her heart beating a tattoo against her ribs, Katherine knelt by the side of the bed and examined Poppy's limbs. To her horror she saw that her legs were covered with a faint but definite purpuric rash. It was one of the signs of meningitis. Worse, it was a sign that the disease had already taken hold.

Forcing herself to keep calm, she ran back to the sitting room and picked up her mobile. Her hands were shaking so badly she was almost not capable of punching in Alexander's number.

To her relief, he picked up straight away.

'Dr Dimitriou.' The sound of his voice almost made her sink to the floor with relief.

'Alexander. Where are you?'

'At home.' He must have picked up the fear in her voice. 'What is it? Are you all right?

'It's Poppy. I need you to come.'

'I'll be there in a few minutes.'

She went back to Poppy's room and tried to rouse her again but once more, her daughter's eyes only flickered. She needed to get antibiotics into her and soon. Perhaps she should have phoned for an ambulance instead of Alexander. But that would take longer. The ambulance would have to come here—at least an hour—and make its way back. And every moment could make a difference.

She sat on the bed and pulled her child into her arms. 'Hold on, darling, please, hold on.'

Alexander was there in less than five minutes, although it felt like hours. He took the scene in at a glance. Katherine looked over at him, anguish etched in every line of her face.

'She feels unwell and has a purpuric rash. I think she has meningitis. Help us, Alexander.'

Although he wanted nothing more than to take her into his arms, he automatically switched into professional mode. He felt Poppy's pulse. Rapid but still strong. She was clammy to the touch but the night was hot. He inspected her limbs and torso. There was a rash but it didn't quite look like the ones he'd seen on patients suffering from meningitis. However, given the recent outbreak, meningitis was still the most likely diagnosis.

'Let's get her to hospital,' he said, picking Katherine's child up. 'You sit in the back with her and phone ahead to let them know we're on our way.'

For once Katherine didn't complain about the way he drove. She cradled her child in her arms, murmuring words of love and encouragement.

Later that night Katherine sat by the bed, holding her daughter's hand. Poppy had been started on IV antibiotics and it would be some time before they would know whether they'd caught it in time. Alexander had disappeared. He was going to phone Liz and Mike as soon as he'd spoken to the doctors again.

Was she going to lose her daughter again when she'd just found her? Why hadn't she forced her to leave even if she'd felt confident that there was zero chance of her daughter contracting the disease? Had she let her own desire to have Poppy with her get in the way of what was right for her child?

She murmured a prayer. 'God, if you're there, please don't take my child. I'll do anything— give up everything—if only you won't take her.'

A few moments later she heard a soft footfall behind her and looked up to find Alexander smiling down at her. Why was he smiling? Didn't he know she was in danger of losing her child?

'I have good news,' he whispered. 'Poppy doesn't have meningitis.'

'What do you mean? Of course she must have. The aches and pains, the rash...'

'It's the rash that got me thinking,' he said. 'It's very like a meningococcal one but I noticed it was only on her shins. I remember reading something about an illness that can mimic meningitis so I looked it up. Katherine, Poppy has Henoch-Schönlein purpura, not meningitis. When the kidneys get involved it can be nasty but Poppy's kidneys aren't affected.'

'She doesn't have meningitis?' Katherine could hardly believe it.

'No. She'll feel quite ill for a week or two, but I promise you she's going to be fine.'

Katherine's vision blurred as Alexander wrapped his arms around her. 'It's okay,' he murmured into her hair. 'You can let go now. I promise you, everything is going to be okay.'

'How is Poppy today?' Alexander asked Katherine a couple of days later when he visited them in hospital. She was a different woman from the one bent over Poppy's bedside when she'd thought her child was desperately ill. The worry and fear had left her eyes and the steely determination he knew so well was back.

'She's booked on this afternoon's flight to London. I'm going with her.'

'Of course.'

'Thank you for being here.' She held out her hand and he grasped her long, cool fingers. 'Thank you for recognising she didn't have meningitis.'

'Will you come back?'

She smiled wanly. 'I don't think so.'

'I love you, Katherine.' She needed to know that.

There was no response. She just looked at him with her cool blue eyes. 'Do you?'

'I was a fool, an idiot-think of any noun you like and it could apply to me, but I love you, more than I thought possible to love another woman. Just give me a chance and I'll prove it to you.'

She smiled wanly. 'I'm sorry, Alexander, but it's over.' She shook her head. 'I need to go if we're to catch our plane.'

He wanted to reach out to her but the coldness

in her eyes held him back. Now was not the time to convince her to give them another chance.

He pressed her fingers. 'If ever you want to come back, if ever you need me, I'll be here.'

CHAPTER NINE

KATHERINE THRUST HER hands deep into her coat pockets and pulled her collar up. Almost overnight, the leaves had fallen from the trees, carpeting the ground.

In a week's time, Poppy would be coming to stay with her for the October school break. Liz and Mike were dropping her off before heading off to stay with Liz's family in the Cotswolds. After Poppy had a week with her, Katherine would drive her daughter up there and stay for the night, before returning to London.

It was amazing how quickly she'd become part of Poppy's family. As she and Poppy had discussed, she never tried to take Liz's place but instead acted the part of the trusted aunt or wise big sister. Poppy had applied to and was starting medical school the autumn after next should she get the grades she and her teachers expected.

Katherine's feet were beginning to freeze as

the cold seeped through her boots, but she was reluctant to return home. The solitude that she'd cherished before she'd gone to Greece—before Poppy and Alexander—now felt disturbingly like loneliness.

The crunch of footsteps came from behind her and she whirled around.

At first she'd thought she dreamed him up.

He was every bit as beautiful as she remembered. His hair was slightly longer and he'd lost weight so that his cheeks were more prominent but laughter still lurked in his eyes.

He was wearing a thick trench coat over a thin jersey and jeans and heavy boots.

They looked at each other for a long moment. 'Katherine,' he murmured, and stepped towards her.

She'd been waiting for him to come to her since she'd left Greece. She'd told herself that he would but she hadn't been sure. Then, as the days had turned into weeks, she'd given up hoping.

What had brought him here now? Her heart hammered against her chest.

'How did you find me?' she whispered.

'You do know that Poppy and Crystal still write to each other? Crystal has been giving me regular updates every time your name is mentioned, which is pretty often, or so I gather.'

But it had taken him all this time to come and find her.

'Is Crystal with you?'

'Of course. I left her at the hotel with Poppy. It was Poppy who told me you'd be here and where to find you.'

'Poppy is in London?'

'She met us at the airport earlier.'

'It sounds as if she's decided to meddle. I think she's frightened I'll stay an old maid and she'll spend her adult years looking after me when I'm an old lady. That's why she asked you to come.'

It was a conversation they'd had as a joke— so why was she repeating it? Why was she babbling?

'Poppy didn't ask me to come, Katherine. I wrote to her and told her I was coming to see you and she asked me to keep it as a surprise.' He stepped towards her, his familiar soapy smell turning her bones to water. 'To be honest, I wasn't sure you'd want to see me.'

She stepped back and he halted where he was. 'How is Grandmother?' she asked.

'Looking forward to seeing you again. I think

she's decided that you are already part of her family.'

Already part of the family?

He took hold of her collar and pulled her close. 'I've missed you,' he said into her hair. 'More than I thought possible.'

'You don't sound too pleased about it,' she mumbled.

'I am. I'm not. It depends.'

She placed her hands against his chest and although she wanted nothing more than to go on touching him for ever, to be held by him for ever, she pushed him away. 'Depends on what?'

'On whether you feel the same way.'

'I think you know how I feel.' She took a moment to steady her breathing. 'But I won't be with you and have you disapprove of me—or of what I did. I can't go through life thinking and feeling I have to pay over and over for what I did.' She tried to smile but it came out all wobbly. 'I've spent the last seventeen years of my life feeling as if I don't deserve to be happy. Being in Greece, being with Poppy changed all that for ever. I did what I felt I had to do at the time. That was the person I was back then and I can't change her. I'm not even sure I want to.'

'God, Katherine. Don't you understand what I'm saying? I love you. I love everything about you and that includes the person you were as well as the woman you are now. When I met you I didn't want to fall in love with you. I tried not to but I couldn't help it. So I told myself that Sophia would want me to be happy, would want me to remarry, especially someone who obviously cared for Crystal.' He looked at her with anguished eyes. 'I didn't tell you everything about Sophia. I have to tell you the rest so you can try to understand why I did what I did.'

He took her hand and led her across to a bench. 'I was six months away from being able to apply for the job in America. In the meantime I had been offered a consultant post at St George's, even though they knew I was going to America. In fact, they said it was one of the reasons they'd chosen me. While I was away they would employ a locum and my job would be kept open for me. It was a flattering reminder of the esteem in which I was held, but at the time I saw it as nothing less than what I was due—what I had worked for over the years.

'But I didn't want to take my foot off the pedal, although I could have. I had the job I wanted—one that was mine for life. I had the post in America. I had done everything I'd set out to do. Now, if there ever was, it had to be Sophia's time. And I was prepared to shoulder more of the child care—or at least that's what I promised Sophia.

'She had an interview for one of the smaller orchestras. It wasn't the career as a concert pianist she'd hoped for but it would have been a start. I wasn't sure. I didn't know if she'd be expected to travel. And it would only have been for eighteen months. But she was so happy to be given the chance. Nervous too. She started playing the piano, practising as if her life depended on it.

'Every hour that she wasn't looking after Crystal she was practising. Often I'd wake up in the night to hear the sounds of Mozart or Beethoven; I can barely listen to their music now. She was in a frenzy—so sure that this was her last chance. It was only then that I realised how much she'd sacrificed for me. And then she fell pregnant again. It wasn't planned, just one of those things, and that was that. Her chance was over.'

He paused for a long moment.

Katherine held her breath as she waited for him to continue.

'It was December and the winter had already been harsh. I left the house early—sometimes before six—but she always got up to see me off. That morning she'd been complaining of a headache. When I think back she'd been complaining of a headache the night before too. But I didn't take too much notice. I was already thinking of a complicated surgery I had that morning. She said she would take some painkillers and go back to bed for an hour or so. Crystal was staying with my mother for a few days. Sophia was thirty-two weeks by this time so I told her that I thought it was a good idea, kissed her and left.' He passed a hand across his face.

'If I'd stopped to look at her, really look at her, I would have seen the warning signs. I was a doctor, for God's sake. A couple of minutes—that's all it would have taken.'

A chill ran up Katherine's spine as she sensed what was coming.

'The roads were bad. The gritting lorries rarely came down the lane leading to our house so I'd taken the four-by-four. She sometimes drove me to the train station so she would have the use of the car, but because she had a headache she suggested I take it. I would leave it at the train station and catch the train from there. It would mean Sophia being without a car, but she said she wasn't intending to go anywhere anyway. She didn't need anything from the village and if she did, she would call me and I could pick it up on the way home.

'I was just relieved to get the use of the car. I needed to catch the six-thirty train if I was to make it to the hospital in time to see my patient before surgery was scheduled to start.'

Katherine's heart was beating a tattoo against her ribs. She sensed what was coming. 'You don't have to tell me any more,' she said softly.

'I do. I have gone over the day so many times in my head, trying to make it come out a different way, but of course that's impossible. We make these decisions in our lives, sometimes ones made in a split second, like the car driver who reverses without looking or overtakes when he shouldn't.'

'And sometimes we agonise over decisions for months but it doesn't mean that they turn out to be right,' she whispered. 'I, of all people, know that.'

'But you've come to terms with your demons. It's taken me this long to come to terms with mine. You need to know what happened so you can try and understand why I reacted to finding out about Poppy the way I did.'

'Tell me, then,' she said softly.

'Surgery that day went like a dream. I had two on my list—both major cases so I wasn't finished in Theatre until late. My secretary had left a note that Sophia had phoned and I tried to call her back, but there was no answer. I assumed she was in the bath—if I assumed anything. I went to see my post-operative patients and planned to try to get her again after that.

'Typically I got caught up and it wasn't until seven that I remembered I hadn't phoned her. I tried again and it went to voice mail. I still wasn't worried. She could be in the bath or in the garden and not heard the phone. She didn't keep her mobile on her unless she was away from home.

'But I was keen to get home—just to reassure myself. I had this uneasy sense of something not being quite right.

'The train seemed to take for ever. I kept trying to get her on the phone and when she still didn't answer I became more and more worried. I wondered if she'd fallen. There was no one nearby—no neighbours for me to call. Sophia would have known their names but I wouldn't even have recognised any of them.

'It did cross my mind to call the police, but I couldn't think of a good reason. My wife not answering her phone for an hour or two was hardly an emergency.

'I collected the car from the station, cursing the snow and praying that the road wouldn't be completely blocked, but nothing was going my way that night. I could only get as close as the lane leading down to the house before drifting snow made it impossible for me to go any further. There was nothing for it but to walk the rest of the way. All this time I was getting increasingly frantic. What if Sophia had gone outside and something had happened? What if she was caught in a snow drift?

'But I told myself that she was too sensible for that. Why would she need to go outside? By that time I was at the house. It was dark—it would normally be lit up like a Christmas tree. It could be a power cut—they weren't infrequent where we lived—but I couldn't fool myself any longer about something being seriously wrong.

'I let myself inside and called out for her. No answer. The lights were working so it wasn't a power cut.

'I found her in our bedroom. She had her mobile in her hand. She was unconscious. But she was alive. I could see that she'd been fitting and now I noticed that her ankles, hands and face were puffy.

'Eclampsia. And I'd been too damn into myself and my career to even notice. But there was no time to berate myself then. If Sophia was to have a chance of surviving I had to get her to hospital and quickly.

'I called 999. They said they would send an ambulance straight away. I told them they wouldn't get any further than my car and that I would meet them there. They said it would take around twenty minutes to get to me, supposing the roads stayed clear. The baby had to be delivered. If I'd had a scalpel with me, so help me God, that's what I would have done.

'She came round briefly, enough to recognise that I was there, but she started fitting again. I waited until she stopped and then I wrapped her in a blanket and carried her to the car. Thankfully the ambulance arrived at almost the same time.

'They delivered our son. But it was too late. For either of them.'

Katherine wrapped her arms around him and held him. What could she say? All she could do for him was let him talk. No wonder he'd been so shocked when he'd found out about Poppy. Sophia had died bringing a child into the world, whereas, it must have seemed to him, she had casually given hers away.

'If it wasn't for Crystal I don't know how I would have got through the next months. In the end it was Helen stepping in that saved us both. As soon as she heard the news she jumped on the first plane. She was with us before night fell.

I was like a madman. That I'd lost the woman who was my very heartbeat was bad enough, but the guilt that she might not have died had I been a different man was worse.

'I stopped going to work. I turned down the consultant job at St George's and the one in America—to be fair to them they told me to think it over, to take my time, but I knew I wouldn't take them up. You see, I no longer felt as if I deserved it. I guess, to be honest, I was sunk in self-pity. So far sunk in it I was wallowing.'

'How old was Crystal?'

'She was three. Old enough to miss her mother but not old enough to understand that she would never see her again and definitely not old enough to understand that this man—who she barely knew, remember—hadn't a clue how to look after her. Even if I had, I was so deep in my trough of self-pity I think I was in danger of enjoying it.

'And when Helen came to stay that gave me more opportunity to wallow. Now she was there to take care of Crystal, there was nothing to hold me back. I drank myself almost unconscious most nights. I rarely got out of bed until mid-morning and when I did I couldn't be bothered getting dressed or shaved. Sometimes I didn't even shower until mid-afternoon.

'God knows how long that would have gone on if Helen hadn't called in reinforcements. It was as if the whole of my extended Greek family had taken up residence. Helen, her mother, my mother and my grandmother too—if my grandfather and father had been alive they would have been there also. I'm pretty sure their disapproving ghosts were in the background, cheering them on and wagging their heads at me.

'Those formidable women kissed and hugged me and then marched me off to the shower. My mother threw every last drop of alcohol down the sink and then Helen and Yia-Yia cooked up a storm. They looked after Crystal, but most importantly they made me see it was my job to care for my child. They fed her and dressed her, but after that it was up to me to look after her.

'Do you know, she clung to them the first time I tried to take my daughter to the park on my own? She gripped the sides of the door when I tried to lift her, so in the end my first trip outside with my daughter since the funeral was with my whole family in tow. It got better after that. I still mourned Sophia but my family made me see that she would have been furious if she'd seen the way I'd gone to pieces. And I knew they were right. I had stolen her dreams from her, and what kind of major creep would I be if I couldn't make a life—a good, loving, caring life—for our daughter?

'The rest, as they say, is history. I sold everything we owned in England and ploughed it into a small practice here in Greece. Then...' he smiled wanly '...I met you. I fought my attraction to you, but I couldn't help it. You were the only woman who had come close to measuring up to Sophia, the only woman I could imagine spending the rest of my life with. But I felt guilty. It seemed a betrayal of Sophia's memory.

'Then I found out about Poppy and it was as if I didn't know you at all. As if the perfect woman I had built up in my mind had disappeared in a breath of wind. I'd put you on a pedestal' you see. I guess we're not so dissimilar, huh? Both of us seemed to feel the need to atone.'

Katherine grimaced. 'I no longer feel I have to atone. As I said, I did what I did and I just have to look at the wonderful young and happy woman Poppy is today to know I made the right decision. I'm sorry I couldn't be perfect for you. But, you know, Alexander, I don't think I want to be perfect.'

'No,' he said softly. 'Of course you don't. You're human. Like us all.'

'So what changed your mind?'

'Nothing changed my mind. When you told me why you gave Poppy up I realised why you'd felt you'd had no choice. And when I saw you with Poppy I could see how you felt about her. I was coming to beg your forgiveness when Grandmother became unwell. As soon as I was sure she was all right I was coming to ask you to stay—to marry me. That's when you phoned me about Poppy. I knew it wasn't the time to tell you how I felt. Every ounce of your attention was—quite rightly—focussed on your daughter. I knew there would be time later—when she was better.'

He rubbed the back of his neck. 'What I wasn't so sure about was whether you could forgive me. Then when you were about to leave and you looked right through me, I thought I had ruined any chance I had with you.' His Greek accent became more pronounced, as it always did when he was emotional.

She looked him in the eye. 'You said you forgave me! I wasn't looking for forgiveness. Not from you! How could I be with a man who thought I needed his forgiveness?'

'It was a stupid, thoughtless thing to say.'

'It was,' she agreed. 'I needed the man I loved to love me warts and all.'

His eyes burned. 'So you do love me?'

'I think I fell in love with you almost from the moment I set eyes on you. But I was frightened too. I wanted to tell you about Poppy but I just couldn't. At least, not then. I was planning to tell you, but then Poppy turned up. I never wanted you to find out that way.

'Then she became ill and I couldn't think of anything else. I thought I was going to lose her again. I made a pact with myself, with the gods, to anyone I thought might be listening. If they'd let Poppy live I would give you up. I know it's crazy but I was crazy back then.'

'But when she was better, why didn't you write to me?'

'It took a long time for her to recover completely. I couldn't leave her.' She smiled wryly. 'And I was keeping my pact. Then when she was completely better I wanted you to come to me. I needed to know that you wanted me. The woman I am, not the one in your imagination.'

'I would have come sooner, but I was arranging a job here. I've taken a year's sabbatical. I love you. I adore you. I don't want a life without you. I lost Sophia because I put my ambition before her needs. I won't do that to you. God, woman, put me out of my misery. I have to know if you love me—if you will marry me and live with me. If you say yes, I'll spend the rest of my life trying to make you happy.' A gust of wind blew the leaves around his feet. But she needed to be sure. She had to know she wouldn't be second best.

'What about Sophia?' she asked. 'I don't want to spend my life competing with the memory of a woman who was so perfect. Because we both know I'm not. None of us are.'

'You're perfect to me,' he said. When she made to protest he stopped her words with his fingertips. 'I don't want perfection, my love. It's too hard to live up to.' He grinned. 'But you'll do me. What about you? Can you put up with a man who doesn't always appreciate a good thing when he comes across it?'

She smiled back at him, her heart threatening to burst from her chest. 'You know what? I rather think I can.'

EPILOGUE

THE TINY WHITEWASHED church was perched on a small promontory overlooking the sea. Poppy had helped Katherine find the place where she would marry Alexander. And it was perfect.

It was a glorious spring day and even the small breeze that whipped Katherine's dress around her ankles was welcome.

Crystal could barely control her excitement. She'd been hopping from foot to foot all morning, keeping up a constant flow of chatter. Poppy wasn't much better. Although she'd tried to hide it, she was almost as excited and thrilled to have been asked to be Katherine's bridesmaid—to the extent that she'd removed her piercings in honour of the occasion, although Katherine had no doubt they'd be back in place tomorrow. Not that she cared. Poppy could have turned up in a paper bag for all she cared. All that mattered was that she was here today, celebrating what was the happiest day of her mother's life.

She glanced at the girls. Crystal with a basket of rose petals hooked over her elbow and Poppy holding the little girl's hand. Who would have thought a year ago that she would be standing here with her two children, because that's how she saw them. Crystal and Katherine had other mothers—women who would always be an important part of their lives—or, in Crystal's case, an important memory, but they had her too. And she would always be there for them—to hold them when their hearts got broken, to help them achieve their dreams, whatever those might be, to support them when life wasn't so kind and eventually to help them plan their weddings, if that's what they wished. Whatever lives they chose for themselves, she'd be there cheering them on, as she was certain her mother was cheering her on. Mum would be so proud.

Her gaze turned to the man beside her, more Greek god than gladiator in his cream suit and neatly pressed shirt. She'd earned her doctorate and had accepted a job in Athens for a couple of years. She was almost fluent in Greek now. After that? They didn't know, but they'd be deciding together.

She had the future—a wonderful future—to look forward to, and she'd be doing it with Alexander by her side.

* * * * *